Mothers Grimm

WITHDRAWN

Danielle Wood is the author of the novel *The Alphabet of Light and Dark*, the short story collection *Rosie Little's Cautionary Tales for Girls* and a biography, *Housewife Superstar: The very best of Marjorie Bligh*. Together with Heather Rose, she is 'Angelica Banks', author of the Tuesday McGillycuddy adventures for children. She lives in Hobart and teaches in the English program at the University of Tasmania.

www.daniellewood.com.au

Mothers Grimm

DANIELLE WOOD

ALLEN&UNWIN
SYDNEY•MELBOURNE•AUCKLAND•LONDON

First published in 2014

*This project has been assisted by the Australian Government through
the Australia Council for the Arts, its arts funding and advisory body.*

Grateful acknowledgement is given for permission to reprint a line from the poem
'Everybody's Mother' by Liz Lochhead from *Dreaming Frankenstein*, copyright © 1984.
Used by permission of Polygon Books. The story 'The Good Mother' was previously
published in *Griffith Review*.

Allen & Unwin
83 Alexander Street
Crows Nest NSW 2065
Australia
Phone: (61 2) 8425 0100
Email: info@allenandunwin.com
Web: www.allenandunwin.com

Cataloguing-in-Publication details are available
from the National Library of Australia
www.trove.nla.gov.au

ISBN 978 1 74175 674 6

Typeset in Mrs Eaves 12.15/17 pt by Bookhouse, Sydney
Printed and bound in Australia by Griffin Press

10 9 8 7 6 5 4 3 2

MIX
Paper from
responsible sources
FSC® C009448

The paper in this book is FSC® certified.
FSC® promotes environmentally responsible,
socially beneficial and economically viable
management of the world's forests.

Nobody's mother can't not never do nothing right.

Liz Lochhead

contents

prologue

the good mother

NOW THAT YOU think about it, you realise you've known her your whole life. On the magazine pages and billboards of your childhood, she was fair as Rapunzel with a shoulder-length haircut. You were indifferent to her, back then, barely registered her presence. Or so you think until you realise you can remember precisely the way her hands looked—their fingernails short and practical though still perfectly tipped with white crescent moons—as she drew V-shapes in menthol rub onto the chests of her ailing children.

She wasn't always the Vicks Mum, of course. Kneeling by the bath, she would soap her toddler's blonde mop into a quiff of white foam and promise you No More Tears. To soothe the unsettled infant, she could provide her favoured brand of paracetamol, as well as the comfort of her pert moulded bosom inside a candy-coloured shirt. With a plump, two-toothed cherub on her hip, she would de-holster a spray pack and vanquish the invisible nasties on the bright white porcelain of her toilets and sinks. For she was the Good

Mother, as safe and mild and effective as every unguent she ever squeezed from a pinkly labelled tube.

The Good Mother had the powders to return muddied soccer shirts to brightness and the potions to ward off sore throats and flu, but you realise now that her true power lay in those hands with their Frenchly polished nails. Remember how she placed them coolly on fevered brows, cupped them around mugs of chocolately-yet-nutritious fluids, splayed them protectively over the shoulder blades of her sleeping babes? Yes, you remember, although it occurs to you only now how implausible it actually was that the peachy boys and girls they found to match her could have been born from her trim blue-jean hips. Come to think of it, where did those children come from? Did Dad ever stop breadwinning long enough for her to rest a hand on the honest chambray of his shirtfront? If he did, you cannot remember it.

This is how it is for the Good Mother. She pricks her finger when she's embroidering. The bauble of blood teetering on her fingertip sets her to thinking, and soon she is noticing the deepness of the red and the way it shines against the snowy ground beyond her window. Add the ravens-wing black of the window frame, and *voila!* She's knocked up and has chosen her child's colour scheme to boot.

This is how it is for you. Deep in denial, you hardly even tell yourself when you stop taking the Pill and start taking folate. Your partner would probably be quite interested if you were to let him know how much better is an unprotected ovulatory orgasm than a regular Pill-protected one, but this knowledge feels for some reason like a secret, so you keep it to yourself. Although you become obsessive about taking your temperature and despite your new habit of cooling your post-coital heels high on the bedhead, there's nothing doing. You get your many test kits from pharmacies in different suburbs so that the sales assistants don't start getting to know you, but no matter how many mornings you lock yourself in the bathroom with a bladder full of potent overnight piss, there's only ever one little line in the window of the white stick.

It's been three years since the rash of weddings in your life, and now it's thirtieth birthday parties. And there she is. Over there by the cheese plate, scooping a strand of fair hair behind one ear and staring down the camembert as if she knows its sole purpose in life is to kill her unborn child. You haven't thought of her for years, if ever you have thought of her consciously at all, which is why you don't recognise her. You say hello and she clinks her water glass against your thrice-emptied champagne flute. Wearing something white, and tight, she sinks into a chair and sighs, and it's only now, as she stretches her hand a full octave across her belly, that you notice her fingernails. They're exquisitely oval and pink as confectionery, each one smoothly iced with white. She gestures at the empty chair beside her and then somehow you are sitting in it.

At all those weddings, people would ask, 'So, what do you do?' Not anymore.

'Do you have children?' she asks, stroking herself as if she is her own pet.

'No,' you say.

'Not yet,' she soothes.

Fuck off, you wish.

'Your first?' you ask, tilting your champagne towards her belly.

'Oh, God no! This is my third.' She laughs and her free hand flies up into the air. When it lands again, it is on your knee. She looks right into your face now and smiles.

'I'm so fertile, my husband only has to *look* at me and I'm up the duff.'

⅗

You make deals with God. You make deals with the Devil. You're not fussy. But as a wise man once said: 'It's the saying you don't care what you get what gets you jiggered.' So you say it, and you're jiggered, but what you give birth to is a hedgehog. It's prickly and its cry is a noise so terrible that you wish someone would scrape fingernails on a blackboard to give you some relief.

You learn that hedgehogs are both nocturnal and crepuscular, but yours doesn't sleep in daylight either. In search of support and camaraderie, you join a mothers' group. You turn up at the clinic covered in prickle-marks and with your squirming hedgehog in your arms. The other women are there already, sitting in a circle nursing their soft, boneless young. The only seat left is beside the Good Mother.

She's wearing pale pink and making smooth circles on her baby's back with her hand-model hands. Things are different since you last met, and you're prepared to forgive her if only she'll tell you how it is that her eyes are so bright and her skin so clear. You're desperate to know how it is that her shiny golden hair is brushed. Clearly her child sleeps, but what is her secret?

'You know what they say,' she says, with a contented smile. 'Calm mother, calm child.'

⌀

One day, you fall into a deep, deep sleep. Valiantly the prince fights his way through forests of fully laden clothes horses, past towers of empty nappy boxes, to reach you where you lie with your rapidly greying hair straggling around your face. He puckers up. His lips brush yours.

'You stupid fucking prick,' you yell at him. 'What the hell do you think you're doing? I only just got to sleep!'

This happens more than once.

Your hedgehog gradually morphs into a child, a boy whose sunny countenance is sufficiently beautiful to make you forget the spines and the sleeplessness. When you conceive again, you are pregnant with the vision of a placid, smooth-skinned human girl child, but what you give birth to—although female—is just another hedgehog.

When Hedgehog II is a year old, your partner announces he is leaving you.

'I think you have a personality disorder,' he says.

'Of course I have a personality disorder,' you say. 'I haven't slept for three years.'

So your partner moves out, just as your maternity leave expires. Your plan had been to go back to work part-time, but now that you're a single mother you have to work full-time to afford childcare for two kids. The economics of this confuse you, but you're too busy thinking about how you're going to manage to worry about that as well. When you go into the childcare centre to make inquiries, your little hedgehog clings to you and makes her sanity-withering cry. The carers hold closer the human children they have in their arms and offer you a three-day trial to settle in your hedgehog before you have to leave her there for real.

On the first day you leave her, she screams until she vomits, so you take her back home. On the second day you leave her, she screams until she vomits, so you take her back home. In a fairytale, things are always different on the third go. But this is life and on the third day you leave her, she screams until she vomits, so you take her back home.

Then comes the day that you are to go back to work. Is that Rumplestiltskin giggling in your mindscape as you hand over both your second-born *and* the bale of hay-spun gold?

The carer takes a tentative hold of your hedgehog. You smile and coo. You turn your back and walk out the door and, as you do, you hear your hedgehog screaming. The effect is like having your uterus torn out through your ear holes. You are sure you can smell vomit.

You only just make it out the kiddy-proof gate before you begin to weep. The weeping makes you red and puffy in the face and now you are hardly presentable for work. In order to pull yourself together, you call in to a café. You open the door and look inside but every table is taken. There's one bar stool but you think perhaps it's the Good Mother sitting on the neighbouring seat and nursing a peppermint tea. You're not certain, but there's something in the blonde foils that makes you wonder and you're in no mood for *her* today. And, besides, by now you're too experienced to fall for her ol' empty-seat routine.

Outside there are no free tables either, but two women who are taking up only half of a large table gesture for you to join them, so you do.

'Thank you,' you say, and they nod in unison.

You take out your fold-out mirror and try to hide the blotches on your face with powder. Then you notice how peachy is the skin of the raven-haired woman sitting on the same side of the table as you. And the skin of the redhead sitting across from her. Each of them has a slim-line pram in a bright, interesting colour. They push their prams to and fro with gloved hands. The gloves are reasonable, aren't they?

It's winter. It's cold. You're telling yourself all of this even though you already know.

No, no!

It's her. Both of them.

And although she's talking to herself across the table, she's really talking to you.

'How old?' one of her asks.

'One,' the other says, with a *can-you-believe-it* manoeuvre of the eyebrow.

'Incredible,' she says. 'I mean, is there *anybody* who thinks it's a good idea to a leave a one-year-old in childcare?'

✺

You take a vow of silence. You will not speak to her. You will not look at her. You will not accept seats at her café table. Out of the corner of your eye you glimpse her, auburn-haired, in a Dettol advertisement, and wonder when you're going to clue up to the fact that these days her hair can be any colour at all?

You tell yourself the consequence of breaking your vow is that your twelve brothers will turn into ravens, or something. In order to hold to your promise you make sudden reversals in supermarket aisles, hide from her in clothing store change rooms, buy bigger sunglasses for their greater protective surface area, teach yourself sign language out of a library book so that if she speaks to you, you can easily pretend to be deaf. You are doing well. Until your eldest child starts school.

You know which is the Good Mother's Volvo. It's the one with the My Family stickers on the back window; she's the one with the handbag and the mobile phone. At first, you think this knowledge will help you to avoid her. You can just make double the number of *Green bottles* when you start singing as you lap the school in your Hyundai, but soon you realise the Volvo is parked multiple times around the perimeter, no matter how early or late you arrive. This is her territory. Here, she is omnipresent.

It's almost Mother's Day and the kids in your son's kindergarten class are given a photocopied page to fill in. Mostly, the page is taken up with a blank square in which each child is to draw a picture, but above the box there's a line of text that is followed by what you will come to recognise as the ellipsis of doom.

I really appreciate it when my mummy . . .

A week later you see the completed tributes where they're pinned up on the wall just inside the classroom. All the figures in the pictures wear bright colours and most have hands pronged with twelve or more fingers. Little Laura reports she really appreciates it when her mummy tucks her into bed at night. For Oliver, it's his mummy's cupcakes. Tara appreciates it when her mummy takes her to the library.

Already you are predisposed to like Clytemnestra, who is a tiny little skun rabbit of a thing to be lugging around the name-equivalent of four suitcases and hatbox. You see that Clytemnestra's had a go herself at changing 'mummy' to 'mummies'. Her picture is a constellation of mint green spots: she appreciates it when her mummies don't cook peas. You are still smiling at Clytemnestra's peas when the Good Mother materialises beside you in her black puffer jacket. She patrols the pin-up board with her eyes.

'Ummm-aaahhh,' she says, happily shocked. 'Look what David's done.'

You haven't yet found your own son's handiwork. And now, even though the Good Mother's manicured index finger is pointing right at it, somehow your eyes are still missing the mark. They are slipping over all the generously endowed hands and circle-striped bellies. You don't want to know.

The Good Mother realises she's going to have to read it out for you.

'I . . . really . . . appreciate it . . . when . . . my mummy . . .' She snickers, *snickers*, before she continues: '. . . buys takeaway.'

Under the sentence, written blackly at your son's instruction by one of the teacher's aides, there is a disturbingly accurate reproduction of the golden arches. You want to protest that you never take him there yourself. It's your ex who does it. And the birthday parties! It's not as if you can say no to these things. Well, not unless you're . . .

The Good Mother interrupts your thoughts with a hand on your upper arm.

'Oh, honey,' she says. 'You must be so embarrassed.'

🖋

Literary scholars view it as a mystery to be solved by careful textual analysis. Psycholanalysts propose theories that involve words like 'splitting' and 'internalisation'.

But you could give them a much simpler explanation.

Yes, you could tell them, couldn't you?

There is no mystery for you.

You could tell them exactly why it is, in fairytales, that the Good Mother is always dead.

lettuce

There was once a man and a woman who longed for a child.
This is not their story.

THIS IS A story about lettuce but it begins with a species of Arnott's biscuit called the Orange Slice, which is a sandwich arrangement involving two fairly plain biscuits stuck together with a disc of orange cream. At the age of eight, Meg had never eaten one, although she had come close. Her piano teacher, Mrs Salmon, used to give out biscuits on a tiny round plate (that Meg was amazed to learn was actually *called* a biscuit plate), which she sat on a painted tea-tray alongside a glass of milk. Sometimes the biscuits were Caramel Crowns and other times they were Kingstons, or—Meg's favourite— Venetians. Once she had eaten her biscuits and drunk the milk, Meg would be expected to settle down at the keys with her *Children's Bach*.

Mrs Salmon, who didn't have children, was both more generous than a mother and less resigned to the inevitable. That is, she was free and easy with the number of biscuits her pupils ate, but a spill of milk on her rug was a cata- strophe. Meg was large for her age, with thickish wrists and undifferentiated knees. By moving slowly and carefully she usually managed to avoid being clumsy, but one day when Mrs Salmon put out the tray with two Orange Slices on the lovely little biscuit plate, Meg reached out rather too quickly to take one and bumped the glass, which teetered, and toppled. At first, the result was a bright white Rorschach blot on the plush patterning of the Persian rug; then it began to sink in. Mrs Salmon was forced to cancel Meg's lesson and Meg had to sit by the door and wait for her mother to pick her up while Mrs Salmon on her knees mopped and scrubbed, the skin inside the collar of her silk blouse turning red and blotchy. And all the while the Orange Slices sat uneaten on the biscuit plate beside the errant, milk-stained glass.

The uncomfortable feelings that Meg began at this time to associate with the Orange Slice were only intensified by a later incident, which took place very early one Sunday morning in the house of the man who lived across the road. A woman and her daughter had recently come to live with the man, a breeder of Cavalier King Charles Spaniels. He had soft curling hair and large dewy eyes and had never before been known to have a lady friend. He kept his many dogs out the back in cyclone-mesh pens that had concrete floors and were easy to hose out. Each pen had a kennel in the corner and each kennel was painted in a pastel shade and filled with charity-shop sheets and blankets that the spaniels dragged out and shredded for entertainment. The woman had bright blonde hair and a powder-blue car but, because she parked it at the top of the man's steep driveway, none of the women in the street had been able to run into her on the footpath and find out what she was all about. Not even Meg's mother had quite enough pluck to turn up at the front door with a tea towel full of scones.

The daughter was called Tracy and she was almost exactly Meg's age, but she was not the sort of girl who took piano lessons. Rather, she went to jazz and tap-dance classes, wore her slippery fair hair in complicated plaits, and had the kind of cheekbones that Meg thought looked excellent when studded with stick-on diamantes. Meg's mother disapproved of jazz and tap, not only because of the quantities of sequins involved, but also because of the make-up and the posing. Meg would not normally have been encouraged to strike up a friendship with Tracy, but Meg's mother seemed willing to tolerate a modicum of bad influence in return for such titbits of information as Meg could, subtly, be encouraged to divulge: Tracy's mother (whose name was Joy) had once won a beauty contest and kept a cut-off plait of her childhood hair in the bottom compartment of a jewellery box; she was a secretary and had painted toenails; she had once been pregnant with a baby that she didn't want so she had it, Meg reported, 'abornted'.

Meg's mother was pleasurably shocked by the fact that Joy obviously confided inappropriately in her young daughter, but was genuinely annoyed by some of the language that Meg was bringing home. For all of her life, Meg had been successfully sheltered from particular words, but since she had been playing jobs with Tracy she had started saying 'agenda' and 'minutes'—words which Meg's mother believed had the power to shape a destiny of deskbound female servitude. These were the days when there was a lot of talk about girls becoming engineers, and Meg's mother was all for that.

On the Sunday morning of the incident, Meg got up much earlier than her parents and decided—still in her pyjamas—to invite herself over the road to play. Tracy in her short nightie opened the door and led Meg into the living room, where *Cattanooga Cats* was on the television. The volume was up very loud. In the bedroom beyond the hall, Tracy's mother sounded as if she were being strangled, but the spaniel man appeared to be suffering equally.

'What are they *doing*?' Meg asked.

'Come here,' Tracy said, and took Meg by the hand into the kitchen.

Tracy opened the pantry in which there were, Meg quickly noted, no ingredients. There was not a labelled Tupperware vat of SR Flour in sight, only packets and boxes and jars and tins of ready-made stuff. Meg couldn't believe Tracy's luck.

'Do you like Orange Slices?' Tracy asked, grinning.

Meg thought of that white blot, seeping away at its edges into expensive Persian silk.

'I love them,' she said.

Tracy grabbed a packet and Meg followed her out the back door into the yard where the dogs leapt and yapped against diamonds of wire. Their runs were strewn with chewed bedding and sloppy whorls of poo, but the smell didn't stop Tracy from kneeling down on the concrete pathway beside the wire and tearing open the cylinder of biscuits. Meg took an Orange Slice from the packet while Tracy picked up the one that had fallen on the ground and shoved it through the wire of the cage. The dogs snuffled and bickered and soon all evidence was gone.

'Are you allowed to do this?'

Tracy shrugged.

'Won't your mum notice?'

'Not if you take a whole packet,' she said.

Meg bit through all the layers of her biscuit (it was nice, although not as nice as a Venetian), but Tracy did something different. She twisted the sandwiched biscuits against each other until they separated. One came off with the disc of cream still firmly attached, while the other one was left plain. Tracy poked the plain one into the muzzle of the nearest dog, and then ate the cream, using her teeth to scrape it off the second biscuit. When she'd finished, the biscuit was soggy and marked with serrated tracks from Tracy's still fairly new incisors. She fed it to the dogs.

'Go on. Try it,' Tracy said.

Meg didn't know Joy very well, so she could only set her level of fear at getting caught on what she knew her own mother would do if she sprang Meg in such a flagrant act of . . . of what? Meg couldn't have said what exactly it was that was so profoundly bad about eating only the cream out of a biscuit, but she knew that it was worse than just the waste.

'I don't really think . . .' Meg started, but Tracy had already given up on her, separated another Orange Slice and begun toothing it clean of its soft centre.

Tracy then proceeded to eat the cream out of the best part of a packet of Orange Slices, while Meg limited her part in the crime to eating three more whole biscuits and feeding some of Tracy's discards through the wire to the dogs. There were, however, no repercussions. Tracy buried the empty Orange Slice wrapper deep in the kitchen bin and, when her mother finally came out of the bedroom with her hair all fuzzed up at the back, it was as if nothing had ever happened.

'Should you be here, Meg?' Joy asked. 'It's very early.'

So Meg went home feeling slightly sick and with her hands smelling of dog, and it wasn't long after this that Joy took up with the spaniel man's brother and they all (except the spaniel man) moved interstate. Tracy and Meg exchanged a few childish letters but their correspondence soon fizzled out. Meg might have forgotten Tracy altogether if it hadn't been for the incident with the Orange Slices, which remained an anomaly in her understanding of the universe.

In the cosmology of Meg, every action had an equal and opposite reaction. Any great good fortune ought to be approached with caution because of the great misfortune that would surely be along at any moment to balance things up. Vegetables were eaten before ice-cream; especially beautiful people were not especially clever, and vice versa; wealth came at the price of creative fulfilment, and the reverse was true, too; women could have big breasts or slender hips, but not both. And Orange Slices entailed the biscuits as well as the cream. Which was why Meg was so affected—Meg more than any of the others—by the woman who did the thing with the lettuce.

There were eleven of them and they were called Meg, Cathie, Kathy, Liz and Libby, Georgie, Lou, Jen, Jo, Mel and Angie because thirty years earlier their mothers had been women of a similar age from the same small town who had understood it as their duty to give their girls sensible and serviceable names with a short form for everyday and a longer form for certificates and special occasions.

In part, it was conscientiousness that brought them together. They were determined to tick every box, to get every part of the experience just right. But perhaps even more than that they were desperate for something to *do* with all that expectant energy—something more active than foreswearing alcohol, avoiding soft cheeses and marking off the passing weeks on the calendar. For most of them, it would be the only time in their lives they would practice yoga.

Their classes were to be held on Saturday mornings at
Roseneath, a mansion on a hillside on the outskirts of their
small town. In its day the old home would have had a circular
driveway and gardens cascading all the way down the slope to
the rivulet, and women would have rustled their skirts as they
stood at the well-positioned bay windows looking out over the
city streets to the harbour. But the view had been built out
decades earlier and the old home's lacy façade despoiled by
the oddly placed metal ramps and stairways that came along
in the years when Roseneath was a maternity hospital.

When Meg learned that the classes were to be held here, she
had to admit there was a certain sort of logic to it. Without its
solid Federation foundations ever moving an inch, Roseneath
had nevertheless managed to follow her around for her whole
life. Meg, along with about half the others, had been born
there. In deck chairs on the upstairs verandas, their mothers
had sat—like passengers on a cruise liner—knitting booties
and nursing their newborns.

After the hospital was closed down, Roseneath was broken
up into tenancies and a group of women started a playgroup
and a toy library in a couple of the downstairs rooms. Meg
had gone to that playgroup and she remembered a photograph
of a bunch of mothers and toddlers—Meg and her mother
among them—all sitting together on the broad sandstone steps
out the front. Everyone was overdressed for the unexpected
warmth of the day, the women flushed in their Viyella dresses
and boots, the children slap-cheeked and paint-smeared in

turtleneck skivvies and corduroy, with haircuts all shaped by the same unisex pudding bowl.

Meg thought of them as she went up the front steps on the day of the first yoga class: those young mothers in the photograph, their hair still vivid shades of red, gold and brown, faces as yet unlined, handmade patchwork nappy bags at their feet. The picture had been taken just before Mother's Day, on an afternoon when the mothers had stayed after playgroup to stretch out a length of canvas on one of Roseneath's downstairs verandas. They had let the children help as they painted a colourful slogan to march behind. *Rights, not roses*, it had said.

In the years since then, Roseneath had housed a succession of fringe causes and services. It had been home to various brands of greenie and peacenik, a theatre company wardrobe, grassroots political candidates and a refugee support centre, among other things. Once, not long after Meg had met Justin, she had slunk into an upstairs tenancy with a jar of her own wee in her handbag. There was so much she hadn't known. For one thing, she'd filled a bulk-sized Vegemite jar for a test that took one or two drops. And she'd been stupid enough to take the words 'Pregnancy Support Service' at face value, not knowing she would be delivering herself for a free anti-abortion lecture. The woman who dispensed the lecture looked at Meg sternly and handed her the negative test strip as a cautionary souvenir.

'What *would* you have done?' the woman had asked, and as usual Meg had said nothing as clever or memorable as she would later wish.

Now, in the hallway of Roseneath, there were posters exhorting Meg to give up smoking, use condoms and be aware of bowel cancer; wire stands bristled with flyers for the building's current crop of fledgling businesses and not-for-profits. The yoga room was at the end of a dog-legged passageway. It was painted in a muddy shade of saffron and had evidently once been half of a larger space: one of its walls bisected a beautiful plaster ceiling rose. There was a sign on the door that said SHOES OFF PLEASE, even though it was clear there was little hope left for the carpet, which was fraying in parts and not especially clean. Upon it a circle had been set, neat as a clock-face, for thirteen.

Each place had its own bolster cushion and tightly rolled mat, and Meg wondered why she hadn't thought, until now, about what the yoga would actually involve. She knew better than to go to fitness classes, where she could never follow the moves and where she always felt oversized in comparison to the jumpy little instructors. But before she could retreat, her friends Cathie and Jen arrived.

This was Cathie's second pregnancy but for all the others it was the first time, and early days at that. As they arrived, in their twos and threes, Meg noticed they shared the habit of fluttering their hands bashfully around their middles. Not that any of their pregnancies was at all scandalous or even secret. Each of the women was married or partnered, although of course it would have been completely fine if they hadn't been. They were modern girls, tolerant and inclusive, and as the weeks went by the straight girls in the group would become increasingly proud of just how proud they were of Georgie and Lou, the gay girls who got themselves knocked up virtually simultaneously after they decided—for better or for worse—to do the whole thing together.

The teacher came through the door and took her place in the circle, and then they were twelve. Meg was momentarily surprised that the teacher was not the least bit Indian, but copper-haired and freckled, perhaps about ten years older than her students. The teacher smiled around the room maternally. Observing one remaining empty place, she frowned mildly and checked her watch.

'Let's just wait a moment or two, shall we?' she said. Then she closed her eyes and affected some graceful move-ments with her hands and wrists. And so they waited—Meg, Cathie and Kathy, Liz and Libby, Georgie, Lou, Jen, Jo, Mel and Angie—and regarded one another, doing their best despite their curiosity to keep their gazes at shoulder level or above.

Meg knew even those of the others that she did not precisely *know*. It was the same for them all: they had either gone to school together or played netball against each other; nicked each other's boyfriends; processed each other's bank loans; booked each other's package holidays; gelled each other's nails;

or fitted little foam moulds full of fluoride to each other's teeth and wiped the dribble afterwards. Meg recognised Mel from behind the desk at her health insurance fund, although today's Mel's ringlets were loose to her shoulders rather than plastered back against her scalp. And opposite Meg was Kathy, whose elbows Meg had known intimately on the high school hockey pitch, but Kathy only sent a cheery little wave across the circle as if everything between them was different now. Which in some ways it was.

If they had not been so already, then they were truly bound together now: a cohort. In six months' time, they would all be wrapped in fluffy dressing gowns and stopping to talk to each other in hospital corridors. Some would be assigned to the same mothers' groups which the health department trusted would cohere sufficiently well that their members would move on from clinic meetings to perambulating together through parks and gardens, and having coffee mornings in each other's homes. But even those who ended up in different groups would now forever more smile at each other over banks of supermarket fruit and vegetables and, on the basis of quick glances, calculate ruthless comparisons of their offspring. Perhaps, as they discreetly checked each other out that day, they had a sense of their shared future, of those distant chilly Saturday mornings when they would be standing on the same, or opposite, sides of a soccer pitch.

She, on the other hand, was nobody they knew. She arrived a good five minutes after the teacher had given up waiting and started the class, by which time the women were sitting with their eyes closed, breathing deliberately.

'In through the nose,' their teacher said. 'And out through the mouth.'

After only a few breaths, Meg began to feel unusual. The breathing lowered her shoulders, loosened the tension in her chest, and now she felt as precarious as a wine barrel with its hoops unbound.

'Take a moment,' the teacher said, her voice making a gentle circumnavigation of the circle, 'to connect with that little life within you.'

The sun was at the window. It fell full on Meg's face so she could see blurred veins on the insides of her eyelids. As she breathed, oxygen poured into her blood and she worried that she might cry.

'Imagine that tiny spine, curled within your womb. Those little fingers, those little toes.'

Who are you? Meg asked of her baby, but instead of any kind of answer she heard the sounds of the door opening, of shoes being slipped off. There was the light scuff of bare feet on the outside of the circle.

Still as a sphinx, Meg opened her eyes to slits and watched a woman take the thirteenth place in the circle. She did it without so much as a mouthed *sorry* to the teacher, or a sheepish glance around the room, and, observing this, Meg felt a disturbance, just a small one, somewhere deep in her own private universe.

Meg studied the latecomer, wondering if the disturbance had been caused by the woman's full breasts and slender hips. Or by Meg's knowledge that, even without the practical limits imposed by time and money, she herself would still have lacked the imagination to invent herself so perfectly as this woman. She wouldn't even have been able to think up the white and low-slung yoga pants the woman wore, delicately frilled at their calf-length cuffs. Or the pale green crop top she'd tied under her bust, leaving her belly bare despite the wintry weather. Meg had worn black leggings and pulled a purple t-shirt down over her fattening stomach, but this woman had exposed the whole of her middle, the slight curve of which was taut and lightly browned, an advertisement of what was to come. *Watch this space.*

There was a word for her but, although Meg could sense it, she couldn't quite pin it down. It had something to do with the woman's lightly bronzed skin, the moonstone on her finger, the silver ring in the shallow swirl of her navel, her long plaits pinned up into a dark-gold crown. The woman stretched her neck and blew an escaping tendril of hair out of her face, and the word hovered at the edges of Meg's mind like an almost-remembered name, its consonants vaguely suggesting themselves. It took Meg a good while to coax the word into focus, but at last she got it and her lips silently secured its shape.

Treasured.

That was it. She had a *treasured* look about her.

Meg thought about the man who would stroke that stretch of belly, and how proud he would be of himself, firstly for having earned the love of such a beautiful woman, and now for having further staked his claim by impregnating her. Not that he would be a husband, this man—that much was clear. He'd be a *partner*. And Meg knew this not because the ring finger of the woman's left hand was conspicuously bare, but because such a woman would need neither to insist on marriage, nor submit to it.

Treasure, he would whisper. *My Treasure.*

Fat guts. That's what Justin had taken to calling Meg as her hips adjusted and her breasts inflated. Or else, *Porky.* They were terms of endearment, though. Often the words went along with a squeeze around her waist, or a bristly kiss on the cheek.

Meg suspected that when Justin had chosen her for his life partner, he had applied much the same logic as he did when he bought a brush-cutter or a ute. He liked things to be solid, well-built, reliable and low maintenance, so much the better if they were cheap into the bargain. Meg had emerged from high school with a low opinion of her solid physique but without any actual eating disorder. At university she had discovered bushwalking and sea kayaking, whereupon she learned to appreciate being taller, stronger and less prone to preciousness than most other girls, although it continued to irk her when petite women strolled through doors ahead of her as if expecting she would defer to them, or worse, hold the door open.

Meg and Justin met on a paddling weekend and, even in their earliest days, she'd taken a certain pride in being an undemanding girlfriend to him. They had married, and opened a plant nursery together, but both as wife and business partner she had never been the sort to ask him to lift a bag of soil or take the garbage out. She couldn't remember ever handing him a jar with a too-tight lid. Meg wasn't sure she would want Justin to suddenly start calling her *Treasure* or *Dearest*, but she wouldn't have minded him noticing the crushing tiredness that was now routinely coming over her late in the day after she'd been on her feet in the nursery since dawn.

One afternoon during the last week, she'd been so exhausted that she hid out in the nursery office where she could shuffle around on a wheelie chair, redistributing unsorted piles of crap. The air in the small room was thick with a meaty smell from the pie Justin had eaten for lunch and there was an overheated whiff coming off the PC. Meg thought she might be sick but shoved the last three squares of a chocolate block into her mouth anyway. Justin put his head around the door.

'You right?' he said. Justin never sat down on the job.

There was a smear of dirt across his chin, which hadn't seen a razor in a week or more. This wasn't bad for business, though. The nursery's main clientele was well-heeled women from the pricey suburb in which Meg and Justin had strategically located their business. They came in—gym-trim in their Levi's 501s and spotless rubber gardening clogs—to fill up their baskets with punnets of pansies and parsley, and Meg saw how much they wanted to take to Justin's grubby, boyish face with a licked corner of a hankie.

'I've ripped out the display garden. Do you reckon you could do it back up again today?' he said.

Meg swallowed. 'Today?'

'Yeah, today. Can't leave it bare. I thought lettuces. Bigger varieties up the back. Pretty, colourful ones down the front. Got to get everyone thinking of spring.'

'But it's only July.'

'Nearly August,' Justin said.

He levered off a gumboot and emptied its mix of sand and pine bark into the wastepaper bin that was right by the door. Odours of ripe sock and warm rubber reached Meg's nose and unhinged her stomach. She caught her chocolately vomit in the nearest empty plant pot, but some dripped out of the drainage holes and onto her lap.

'Shit, you right?' said Justin, rushing at her with the bin.

Meg gulped a few times, tried to normalise her breathing. She wished someone would get her a bowl of stewed apricots.

'I'm okay.'

'Oh, it's the . . . ah, thing,' he said, pointing to his stomach.

One boot on, one boot off, he strode away and a minute was back with a roll of paper towel from the front counter. He held the bin while Meg wiped her face and her trousers.

'You right now?' he said.

She wanted to lie down, even if it was on the grimy office lino with the phone book for a pillow.

'Yep.'

He mussed her hair affectionately, then said: 'There's a bunch of extra lettuce seedlings up in the top potting shed.'

⁊

The second yoga class began as the first had done, with a single empty space in their circle. This time, though, the teacher did not ask the others to wait, but invited them to close their eyes, set aside their thoughts and be present within their bodies.

'Feeling your breath's flow, allow yourselves now to be still,' the teacher said. She inhaled strenuously, nostril-wise, and her students did the same.

Then Treasure arrived, her hair loose this time. It was even longer than Meg had imagined, curling all the way down to her lower back in a state of artful dishevelment. The dress she wore over matching leggings was grey-green and stretchy, clinging so closely to the tiny curve of her pregnant belly that Meg could make out the outline of her navel ring beneath.

The dress had a wide boat neck that stretched almost shoulder to shoulder and, as Treasure sat down, Meg glimpsed a strap of pistachio-coloured lace and cream velvet.

She knew that bra. She knew the brand, and the cut of the matching panties, and the price, because there was only one boutique in their small town that specialised in maternity wear, and she had gone there one afternoon, against her better judgement, when she had slipped out of the nursery to do the banking. The boutique was housed in a converted cottage that was painted in shades of oatmeal and had rooms smelling of vanilla. In the lingerie room there was nothing but a velvet-curtained change room and a two-tiered carousel which had reminded Meg of a cake stand at high tea. The garments were like pastries in their shades of cream, mocha, raspberry and chocolate—iced with embroidery, piped with narrow velvet, cased in lace—and Meg became uncomfortably aware that her nipples had tightened as if reaching out to them.

As Meg lifted out a confection of pistachio lace and velvety cream, the sales lady came into the room and put on a show of searching the change room for unwanted items, as if she were not really checking up on Meg and the big fat handbag she had wedged in her armpit like a goose.

'Pop that in the change room for you, love?' she said, holding out a hand, and the hint of accusation was enough to give Meg—who never even thought of stealing anything—a little rush of guilt. Meekly, she handed over the bra.

In the change room were posters, and in the posters were women with hair pinned up and loose curls straying, their mouths half-open, eyes half-closed. Full cream breasts strained against ribbon and lace, pretty panties underlined bellies as big and round as steamed puddings. Meg tried on the bra and she didn't even need to look in the mirror to know that she wanted to own the way the firm green cups smoothed her breast flesh, and the way the lace embellished her cleavage. When she leafed over the price tag, the staggering figure made her feel sick, so she had dressed back in her own clothes and handed over the bra to the sales lady, who was not in the least deceived by her promise to *think on it*.

'As you breathe in . . . put one hand on your heart . . . and breathe out. Rest your other hand on your belly,' the teacher said. 'Each time you breathe in, you are taking in the oxygen that sustains your baby's life. Remember you are breathing not for one, but for two.'

Meg, glancing across the circle, made note that the moonstone was gone from Treasure's middle finger, replaced by a princess-cut diamond in a proud vintage silver setting. Meg imagined the jewellery box that Treasure would have in her wardrobe, or perhaps on a dressing table in front of a big oval mirror. She imagined its antique tangle of silver and rose gold and white gold and pretty stones, and Meg knew that Treasure's partner would never say 'What for?' when asked, over the breakfast bar one morning, if he would like to put the eleven-week ultrasound appointment date in his diary.

Treasure would never need to press him, so he would have no cause to slap her lightly on the haunch and say, 'Come on, Pork Chop, don't go getting all pathetic on me.'

It occurred to Meg, after Justin had said that, to tell him that she didn't so much want him to come to the appointment as she wanted him to want to come. But when she tried that out in words, it sounded like the kind of manipulative manoeuvre that a truly pathetic woman might make. *Was* she pathetic? The word had stung. And, to make matters worse, Meg remembered reading—in a magazine, probably, or else one of those best-selling books for women that Meg's mother-in-law bought for herself and then passed on to Meg—that the criticisms which hurt the most were those that you believed, deep down, to be valid.

'Pathetic' had long been one of Meg's mother's favourite words. It was for women who too obviously enjoyed breast-feeding and who fussed over children's bruised knees instead of saying 'up you get and rub it better'. It was for mothers who indulged in teary goodbyes at the school gate, and pregnant women who expected to have their feet up all the time and people bringing them cups of milky tea.

'Keep running with the tribe,' Meg's mother was fond of saying, especially now that Meg was pregnant.

This exhortation was the text of a telegram that Meg's mother had got from her father, Meg's grandfather, right after Meg's birth. It had to do with the supposed facts relating to women of unspecified nomadic tribes, and what they did if they had to give birth during a long, migratory march. According to Meg's grandfather, these women would duck off behind a rock and squeeze out their babies with no more fuss than if they were having a bush wee. Therefore, post-partum women who malingered in hospital were, in Meg's mother's view, 'pathetic'.

Was there anything pathetic, though, about wanting the father of your child to come along to the first ultrasound of your pregnancy? It was only an ordinary miracle, but it was theirs, and Meg had thought that Justin might want to witness it. It wasn't as if she expected to be congratulated, or thanked. Meg had heard of men being grateful, even buying emerald rings and diamond necklaces for the women who had borne their children. But Meg thought it unlikely that such a thing happened any more. Except perhaps to women who had jewellery boxes and oval mirrors and golden hair tumbling down past their beautiful breasts to the tops of their slender thighs. Ordinary women, she thought, were probably just thankful if they could find a man who was happy enough to inject the raw materials and live with the consequences. Because children, as Justin's mates who were already fathers had pointed out to him, and as he in turn had pointed out to Meg—and this was after Meg had conceived—were completely pointless. They were expensive, tied you down, kept you up, and then never left home.

Meg had thought about all this as she sat, alone, in the waiting room at the imaging centre. She had thought about it while she lay on the narrow stretcher bed and while, on the screen, in place of her miracle, a creature waggled its oversized skull and fleshless limbs like something rubbery and fluorescent you might hang in your doorway at Halloween. By the time she stood at the reception desk with her credit card in hand, she couldn't remember why she was pregnant in the first place.

$\mathcal{D}$

'Actually—' said Cathie, leaning in confidentially. Then she fell silent as the waiter arrived with their drinks.

Cathie and Meg had gone out for coffee after yoga. They still called it that—'coffee'—although they wouldn't have dreamed of consuming caffeine in public. Meg had gone straight to the café while Cathie had gone via her mother's to collect the baby. It was a small, popular eatery that had sprung up quite unexpectedly on a suburban street which had little else to recommend it. Even though it was winter, they took a seat outside, where—at regular intervals along the pavement—white-trunked saplings seemed to sprout directly out of the concrete.

They chose an outside table in part because of the pram—which reminded Meg of a spaceship with its lime-green escape pod and its clever, lightweight frame—and in part because the café was busy indoors and they didn't want to lower their voices the way you have to in a small town. Meg and Cathie had begun by agreeing it was a shame Jen couldn't come this day. She had an appointment with her dietician, apparently, and Cathie and Meg spent some time wondering if it was really for the best that Jen was still following her strict vegan regime while pregnant. With this item covered off, their talk turned to Treasure.

Towards the end of the class, the teacher had asked the women to form pairs for a pose called the One Foot Prayer. It had been important to find someone roughly your own height, and Meg had been in equal parts relieved, envious and unsurprised that it was Cathie who had found Treasure.

Meg and Cathie had known each other for a very long time. In early primary school their class had gone on a bus to another school that was out in the bush and where the children had chickens in pens and tended vegetable plots which had leeks and kale and other vegetables little Meg had never heard of. They were to pair up—one child from the city, one from the country—and the country children would teach the city children to bake bread. It was left to the children to find their own partners: boys wanted boys and girls wanted girls, but Cathie had wanted one particular girl, the prettiest one. This girl had been pretty after a simple storybook fashion: fair plaits and large blue eyes and pink cheeks and Cathie had lunged with indecent speed to claim her, grabbing her and holding on tightly so that nobody else could get her. Meg remembered there had been a big fuss when the girl cried out in pain and showed the teachers the livid crescent moons made on her wrist by Cathie's fingernails.

While Cathie and Treasure had balanced and stretched, Cathie had deployed her Girl Scout smile and kept up a flow of effortless chat and Meg had been dying to know what they were saying.

'So, actually—' said Cathie, beginning again.

'Yes?' said Meg.

'She's single,' Cathie said.

'What?' Meg's question came out with a derisive little snort that she had not intended.

'Uh-huh. Not married. Not in a relationship. Single. Not that there's anything wrong with that, of course,' Cathie said.

Meg tried to remember how to spell that German word. Was it with a *fraud* for fake, or a *freud* for Sigmund?

A small noise came from within the pram. The baby, a girl, was not yet a year old, but it was typical of Cathie that she was already onto her second, which of course would be a boy. Pigeon pair. Done and dusted. Cathie had already booked in to have her tubes tied straight after the birth.

'So, she just came out and told you that?' Meg said.

The noise escalated and Cathie made a shushing sound as she shunted the pram back and forth over the pavement. Meg didn't doubt for a second the baby would go back to sleep and stay that way until Cathie was ready for her to wake up. Meg could picture what Cathie would be like with her children when they were older; she could already hear the lovingly bossy register that Cathie would specialise in but that Meg would never be able to find.

'I only asked her if her partner was happy about the baby,' said Cathie, expertly adjusting the blanket she had draped over the front of the pram. 'And I said "partner". I didn't say "husband" or "bloke". And she said she was on her own.'

'Then who *is* the father?' Meg blurted. She blushed, realising she had sounded almost angry.

'Jesus, Meg,' said Cathie. 'I'm good, but I'm not that good.'

🕊

It was a struggle for Meg to let go of Treasure's partner. To replace him she had thought up a few different options. Perhaps an unscrupulous married colleague who had knocked up Treasure in a lunchtime hotel room. Or had it been a muscle-shirted youth dragged unwittingly home from the pub? Or, perhaps more likely, a long-time friend and sensitive guitar-playing poet who had always wanted more from their relationship and had nobly agreed to come to the party. Each Saturday at yoga class, Meg watched carefully for clues to which one of them had done the deed, but if pushed she would have had to admit that she was never convinced by any of them.

Meanwhile, in the nursery, spring came, bringing with it the part-time and first-time gardeners, their legs bright winter white in the stretch between khaki shorts and elastic-sided boots. They bought basket-loads of vegetable seedlings, or a whole driveway's worth of lavender and box. Young couples would struggle up to the counter with a heavy potted tree between them and Meg would almost be able to see, in the air above their heads, their shared visions of that tree's branches shading their daughter's wedding day, holding a cubby house for their grandchildren, shedding its crispy golden leaves over their ruby wedding anniversary celebrations.

In Meg's display garden the icebergs were building their own hearts, inner leaves folding like pale green hands around a secret. The deep green leaves of the winter density were beginning to scrunch up and look brainy, while the lamb's ear proliferated in small, furry lobes. Buttercrunches bloomed in soft, open roses and speckles freckled the shiny flanks of the flashy trout back. Meg watched over her lettuces, plucking off slugs and snails, searching beneath the spreading crinolines of the oakleaf, and the blood-brown lace of the mignonette, for weeds. She would yank these out and fling them aside along with their webs of thread-thin roots.

Meg and Justin always saw a spike in sales of the plants they featured in their display garden, but this spring their lettuce sales were unprecedented, and it brought up one of Meg's old chestnuts—the one about the morality of the nursery business. She wondered if it were honest to charge people so much for lettuce seedlings they could easily—with the invest-ment of a week or two—have grown themselves from seed. It troubled her, too, the amount that people would spend on plants for which they had not the right soil, nor the expertise to nurture, nor the dedication to water, and she wondered if it were right to profit so handsomely from their cycle of ambition and failure. On a good day in spring, the queue to the checkout ran the full length of the display garden, and Meg at the cash register took people's money and tried not to think too much about the fate of the plants going out the door all green and glossy and hopeful.

🖙

'Standing up, if you wouldn't mind, ladies,' the teacher said.

By now the women had grown quite a bit larger and, as they stood up in their circle, Meg heard the faint sounds of knees and hip joints cracking.

'And find yourself a partner.'

Meg searched the room and located Treasure, her hair in low, loose pigtails that came forward over each shoulder. If Cathie could do it, then surely so could she, although Cathie would just know what to say and how to say it without having to think it all out first the way Meg did now. She thought she could probably ask, *When's your due date?* That was a safe question. *Do you know what you're having?* Nosier, but Meg would have thought acceptable under the circumstances. *Have you chosen a name?* That was probably off-limits.

Meg moved towards Treasure, but before she had taken more than a few steps, Meg was found and claimed by Kathy of the formidable elbows, and Treasure had partnered with Angie.

'Standing face to face, and take hold of each other by the forearms,' the teacher said. 'Look into your partner's beautiful face and smile. That's it. Now bend your knees and lean backwards. Trust your partner to support you as you feel that stretch coming into your legs. We're going to need strong legs, ladies. Standing up can be a wonderful position for birthing.'

Meg and Kathy took each other's weight and eased into a crouch, bellies sliding down between their solidly planted thighs. *Every action has an opposite and equal reaction*, Meg thought, grateful now that it was Kathy and not Treasure who had the task of holding her by the forearms.

'By now, you'll feel some discomfort in your legs,' the teacher said. 'But all you need to do is take your mind away from that. There's no need to get involved. Instead, I want you to focus on your inner sunflower. It's very bright, very yellow. And it will be there to smile at you, all the way through your labour, if only you care to look for it.'

This was an easy exercise for Meg. She liked sunflowers and the pain in her legs, if she was truthful, was not particularly bad.

'So, now we're saying thank you to our partners, and moving back into the circle. Thank you, ladies. I think we all know each other well enough now, don't we, to have a little fun together? So, let's all take our right hand and place it down here on the pubic bone, like so.'

The teacher touched herself firmly between the legs, her womanly backside thrusting out behind her as she shaped her body into a half-squat. Her students made their bodies into timid copies.

'And the left hand goes here, right down here, at the tailbone. Now, experiment with how it feels as you make a scooping movement with your pelvis. Stick your bum right out. That's it. Like a big baboon bum. Now rotate forwards, like so. Bum out, scoop forwards. And again. Lovely.'

Meg felt the class split itself in two. There were those who didn't care that they looked ridiculous, and those like her who wished they didn't care, but couldn't help it. Meg glanced, as had become her habit, at Treasure. But Treasure was not, for the moment, being a baboon. Her hair had come loose and she was twisting its length, bundling it into an exquisitely messy knot at the nape of her neck.

'Now, keeping up the scooping, we're going to take a walk,' the teacher said. 'I call this the camel walk. Let's go clockwise, shall we? Scoop. Scoop. That's it! Beautiful! Don't bump into each other, camels!'

Meg wished she were one of the uninhibited camels humping their way in ungainly circles around the room, but all she could do was draw in the limits of her peripheral vision and try to console herself with the idea that nobody else was looking at her, just as she was looking at nobody else. This didn't help very much. Her cheeks burned. By the time she was halfway through the first lap, the only thing standing between Meg and conscientious objection was the certain knowledge it was actually less mortifying just to get on with the business of being a camel than it was to draw attention to herself by stopping.

Camel-wise, Meg approached the window side of the room, aware of the way her heavy footfalls caused little tremors in the floorboards beneath the carpet. The room was fairly dark and the window small but it was catching in full the morning sun, making a bright patch in Meg's narrowed field of vision. She lurched towards the window, the sun so dazzling that it took a moment for Meg to register the form of a slender woman, standing, leaning up against the wall beside the window, the sole of one bare foot resting against the calf of her other leg.

Was this allowed? Meg looked around for the teacher and found her, camel-walking in cheerful clockwise circles, swinging her pelvis on the fulcra of her thigh bones and Meg suspected that she was deliberately not noticing Treasure standing by the window. Without exactly deciding to, Meg took matters into her own hands.

'Not joining us?' she asked, smiling what she hoped was an inclusive smile.

You might almost have said that Treasure shook her head, but she didn't exactly: by way of a barely perceptible movement of her eyes and her neck, she made a tiny gesture of disinclination. And Meg, quite unreasonably, she knew, felt like slapping her flawless face.

ᘓ

Over coffee, with sudden inspiration, Cathie said, 'Oh, my God. Maybe she's a surrogate? The way she dresses, there's no shortage of money.'

'No,' said Meg. 'I thought of that.'

'You're right. Too princessy,' Cathie said. 'I'd love to see her in labour. It's not like you can just wander over to the window to have a rest from *that*.'

Jen scooped a spoonful of soy milk froth off the top of her hot chocolate and put it in her mouth. Of the three of them, Jen was furthest along in her pregnancy and, when Meg thought of Jen's future, she imagined kids with runny noses who were perpetually on homeopathic drops of some kind.

Jen was possessed of the mild hypochondria that in Meg's experience often went along with being a nurse. There was frequently a test result pending, or special exercises to be done. Jen was equally interested in other people's complaints, though. To Meg she had recommended any number of Bach flower remedies, chiropractors and Bowen therapists, and Meg sometimes wondered what was wrong with her because she never really felt she needed anything more than a Panadol and an early night. Meg had Jen pegged as one of those gentle sing-song mothers: endlessly sympathetic, but all whispery and defeated in the face of a tantrum.

What about herself, then? It was only fair, now, that Meg have a deprecating thought about herself, just to even things up. Well, she'd have a boy. That much was certain. Surely that's what these walloping great hips were for: pushing out strapping, unexceptional, but reasonably compliant boys who would heft wheelbarrows around the nursery and help stack the back row of a rugby team. And what kind of mother would she be? She tried to summon a fault. Lazy? No, not really. Grumpy? Rarely. Boring? Yes, that was most likely it. She'd probably have boys with natures in the same undemonstrative ball park as Justin's and she'd be the sort to insist on them kissing her goodbye when they were off to do things more interesting than be with her, and they'd do it, too, but only because they felt they should.

'A one-night stand then?' Cathie said. 'Accidents can happen to anybody.'

The waiter passed with a tray of drinks for another table and the rich smell of coffee made Meg's lemon and ginger tea taste even more like the overpriced hot water that it was. Jen, still with the spoon in her mouth, said nothing.

'But if it was just that, an accident, why wouldn't she have an abortion?' Meg said.

'Maybe she's Catholic.'

Jen was saying nothing, but it was killing her and eventually Cathie noticed. Cathie leaned back in her chair and smiled. 'Really?' she said.

The part of the hospital in which Jen worked was fertility. In some kind of put-on accent, Jen said, 'I say nothing.'

Cathie gave a little laugh but Meg was confused.

'She's a patient of Jen's,' Cathie explained,

'*Is* she?' Meg asked.

'I can't tell you that. I could lose my *job*.'

'What are we talking here?' said Cathie. 'Artificial insem-
ination? From someone she knows?'

Sweeping back past them with an empty tray, the waiter
asked, 'Can I get you ladies anything else?'

'Uh-uh,' said Jen, shaking her head.

'You're saying donor sperm, then? The off-the-shelf
stuff?' Cathie asked.

'Was I talking to you?' said Jen.

Meg only stared. Then she blinked, and Treasure's
colleague and her muscle-shirted youth, along with the poet
and his guitar, fell away. If Treasure was Meg's cardboard doll,
then she was back to wearing nothing more than the white
pants and singlet she came with. Meg had tried pinning to her
every single thing she could imagine: loneliness, desperation,
bereavement. None felt right. The only thing she had almost
managed to make stick was a vision of Treasure's home: an
apartment, small and somewhat gloomy, with nothing but a
cactus on the kitchen windowsill and perhaps a tomato plant
on the balcony if you were lucky.

※

Spring turned to summer, and lettuce sales continued to
flourish. Since the profit margin was so high, Justin asked
Meg to keep up a rolling planting schedule, plucking out the
older lettuces when they began to look shabby and settling
fresh specimens into their places. Meg sent away for lettuce

seed of yet more different kinds: varieties that you could sell to younger gardeners because they were old and authentic, and ones that you could sell to older gardeners because they were new and improved.

Meg's belly grew firmer and rounder, developing an unambiguous shape that made it quite safe for comment. Soon there was something cartoonish about its contours, especially from side-on; in the mirror in her nursery uniform, she had become Mr Greedy made green. She had read all about how people had the idea pregnant women were public property, and she knew she was supposed to feel offended and invaded when strangers reached out to touch her on the stomach, but the truth was that she quite liked it. It was only the same as people wanting to pat dogs in the street because the dogs in the street reminded them of the dogs they had at home, or because they just really liked dogs. Meg couldn't see the harm in it really. Maybe there was some way in which she was strange, or wrong—perhaps she hadn't read as far as the part that explained why—but when an elderly man set his bottle of citrus food down on the nursery counter, shaped his crooked hands to her belly and whispered, 'Good on you, love', she felt as if she had both given and received a blessing.

'Are we finding out, or having a surprise?' the sonographer asked Meg during a scan, pausing with her gluey handpiece on Meg's stomach.

'It won't be much of a surprise,' said Meg, cheerfully enough.

'You think you know already?' The sonographer arched an eyebrow.

'Yes,' said Meg. 'That's a boy in there.'

'You wouldn't believe how many people come in here certain that they know, and leave with a whole new paint scheme in mind.'

For a split second, a little girl blossomed in Meg's imagination. She had dark hair like Meg's, and Justin's long eyelashes, although Meg was realistic enough to give her a chunky torso and dimpled knees. But before long the sonographer, moving layer by layer in cross-section through the foetus, came upon the shape of testes and a penis. Meg's baby girl burst like the bubble she always was.

Nevertheless, these were good days and good enough that Meg was able to recognise them on their first pass, not even having to wait for hindsight. The more her belly grew, the greater was her sense of herself as a gigantic, benevolent bee, hovering fatly around the plants in the nursery, having the power to coax out their shoots and buds and runners. The depth of her hunger made food taste better and the rich smells of the nursery seemed to have opened out into new dimensions. The perfumes of the flowers were now so strong and complex that Meg came to truly understand wine critics' use of the word 'bouquet'. She could sniff the layers of meaning in loam and in sand, and found herself unscrewing the caps of seaweed fertiliser to drink in the marine stench, delving a hand into blood and bone fertiliser to stir up the rich, dark stink of life and death and rot and promise, although, even as she did so, it occurred to her that it was probably written down somewhere not to do that when you were pregnant.

✆

Soon, it was Meg's birthday.

'The last,' her mother had said, 'that will be all about you.'

'Rubbish,' said Justin's mother. 'We'll always make sure it's your special day, even when that gorgeous boy is here. Now sit down, love, and put your feet up. I'll get you a cup of tea.'

'I'm fine thanks. Really,' said Meg, although if her own mother had not been there, she would have accepted, gratefully.

Justin's mother had given her a very special present: a gift voucher for a Sylvie Arlington photo shoot. There were Sylvie Arlingtons—huge, grainy close-ups of navels and nipples and mouths and hands and feet—in the maternity floor reception area of the private hospital through which Meg had taken a tour, and where she was booked for pre-natal classes. Justin's mother had put a lot of money down on the voucher, enough for the deluxe package that included both pregnancy shots and mother-baby shots later on. Meg thought—and then gave herself a mental pinch for it—that a series of Sylvie Arlingtons would soundly trump Cathie's photos.

Cathie had shown the pictures to Meg at Jen's baby shower. Jen, having decided against photographs, had bought a DIY kit and made a plaster belly-cast which had been the centrepiece at the shower tea, standing on a coffee table and reminding

Meg of a Venus de Milo with even fewer extremities. Around the base, Jen had put out paints and oil pastels so her shower guests could cover the cast with flowers and benedictions. Her idea was that it would eventually be filled with plants and used as a courtyard feature.

Meg leafed through Cathie's pictures and made all the appropriate comments.

Cathie had a sister who owned a good camera and had done a year at art school, but part of the problem was that Cathie had roped her husband into the shoot. Although he'd done all the things he was told—like reaching around his wife's belly and making his forefingers and thumbs into a heart shape around her navel—he hadn't been able to get rid of the embarrassed look on his face. Then there was a series of shots in which Cathie was alone and lying naked on the sheet-covered couch, a swathe of faux fur emphasising her nearly full-term belly, a slightly lewd look on her face. Meg noticed the little flaws in the shots, like the light switch in the top corner of the frame, and the triangle of couch fabric that showed where the sheet wasn't pulled up quite properly. But these weren't the only thing—or even the main thing—that was wrong with the photos. The real issue, Meg thought, was that you could see how each of the pictures was meant to have looked, but not one of them actually did.

Not long after her birthday, Meg rang the number on the voucher and made an appointment to meet with Sylvie Arlington's assistant. She was a slight young woman with statement spectacles and she showed Meg through the studio—a white room with huge casement windows and heritage floorboards, beyond which was a formal garden—before sitting her down in a study furnished with nothing but a desk, a chair and a screen. The assistant brought Meg a cup of herbal tea and set going a slide show of images in order for Meg to get a sense of her options.

Most of the images were black and white, or sepia-toned, although some of them had accents in baby pink, lemon and blue. Meg supposed it was easy to make babies look like models, but Arlington had caught all of the women at their best, too. She clearly knew all the clever ways of showing women's bodies without making them uncomfortable about their nakedness. There were diaphanous wraps and carefully crossed legs, arms over nipples.

And then there she was. Treasure. On the screen. There were several shots of her and in none of them was there even a scrap of chiffon. She stood utterly naked in the studio, looking down at her pregnant belly, her hair completely loose and falling down her back. Arlington had shot the full, lithe length of her from the side, from the front, from behind. As frame replaced frame, Treasure moved relatively little. She lifted one knee so that her toe was on pointe, clasped her hands together behind her buttocks, arched her back. And then she was gone, replaced on the screen by a gaptoothed woman who had elected, possibly unwisely, to be photographed with a garland of daisies in her hair.

When the assistant returned, Meg did make an appointment with Sylvie, for new publicity shots for the nursery. No matter the extent of Sylvie Arlington's skill, Meg knew there was nevertheless a fathomless divide between a sow's ear purse and one made out of true silk. She just hadn't worked out quite how she was going to tell Justin's mother.

✻

Before long, the songs being piped through the supermarkets and shopping centres were all about a baby and a birth and Meg, while standing in queues, found that people with shopping baskets full of tinsel and gift-wrap would smile at her kindly. And knowingly. *Just you wait.*

In the nursery it was the season for small pots of mistletoe, for tub-bound conifers and for the poor old poinsettias that would brighten the Christmas table and then most likely get binned with the shredded remains of the bon-bons.

The yoga school was winding up for the break and this would be the last of their classes. Already, the circle was somewhat diminished: Libby had been the first among them to give birth, closely followed by Mel, and then Jo. By the end of the exercises the women were sheeny with sweat and they lolled on the fraying carpet like so many gestating seals.

'Well, beautiful blossoming ladies, have you any final thoughts to share with each other today?' the teacher asked.

Meg watched the women shift about in response to their teacher's question, postures opening up or closing down, introverts and extroverts silently declaring themselves. It was something Meg and Treasure had in common that they never said anything during these opportunities for open discussion.

'I wasn't going to find out, but at the last scan I couldn't help myself. I'm having a girl,' said Kathy.

'I had a text from Jen this morning,' Cathie announced. 'She's almost certain she's in labour.'

'My sister's just found out that she's pregnant, too,' said Angie.

'My baby's going to be early. We're trying to work out what to do if we go into labour on the same day,' said Lou, gripping Georgie's hand tightly.

'My doctor told me my baby is going to be big. Apparently, he's going to be very big,' said Liz, although the fear on her face was nothing more than the delighted terror of a child outside a house of horrors. Meg, like all the others—except Cathie—had no way of knowing precisely how much fear was required, but she knew it was more than this.

'And how do you feel about that?' the teacher asked Liz.

'Like I might need to plan for a caesarean,' Liz laughed.

'That's one way to think,' the teacher mused, 'although another is to remember that a big healthy baby boy will have the strength to help you, to support you, through natural birth. Does anyone else have any thoughts on this?'

Meg knew that most of the women in the circle had written out birth plans and had strong views on which would be the most suitable positions, on pain relief and on what they wanted to happen immediately post-partum. Meg had not written a plan, but she had read enough to know that considering a caesarean was something you didn't do out loud in public. Meg had been over at her parents' house during the week when it had come on television that a study had found women who had caesareans were less responsive to the sound of their own baby crying than women who had birthed naturally.

'Honestly, who funds research like that?' Meg's mother had muttered. 'Pathetic.'

'Anyone?' said their teacher.

For Meg there was pregnancy, and there was holding a baby in her arms; the territory between was nothing but cloud and fog. But it seemed that this time Treasure had something to say. She leaned forward a little, her bare brown belly resting on her thighs, navel ring glowing dully against her skin. She spoke seriously, perhaps a little fervently.

'I'm really committed to giving birth naturally. I want to have the full experience, even the pain.'

The teacher smiled approvingly and Meg felt a ripple of consensus lap the circle, although she noticed it skipped over poor, silly Liz.

'Let's finish then, shall we, with our breathing?' the teacher said. 'Close your eyes now, and look deep within yourself. I want you to see your heart now. See it opening, opening up to your baby. Let your heart swallow your mind.'

Meg watched Treasure's eyelids fall closed over her inscrutable eyes, and wondered what it was that she saw. When her own eyes closed it was upon a vision of the blackness of space, an infinite expanse of swirling galaxies and distant planets and invisible dark matter, a universe of tugging gravities in which the weights and measures refused to resolve to her satisfaction.

⚯

It had been part of the concept, when Meg and Justin started the nursery, to make it feel like a world unto itself. To this end, there were rendered walls covered with espaliered roses and fruit trees, canopies threaded with a leafy mix of grape and passionfruit vines, and—in places where permanent walls could not be built—there were high tea-tree screens and rows of potted conifers to keep out the visual aspects of the surrounding shops and roads, even if the noises of them slipped through.

Meg had not so much as lifted a paintbrush or glued a frieze in the room that was to be their baby's, but as she wandered up and down the planted aisles, between the herbs and seedlings and ground covers and natives, she began to imagine what it would be like to do the same with her baby in a sling across her front, or, later, in a pack upon her back. It was within the vegetable walls of the nursery, far more than within the rooms of her own home, that Meg felt the presence of a nesting instinct. Even so, Meg had never considered that the nursery was a place in which she felt territorial, exactly. Which is why it took her by surprise, the sudden surge of primal rage she felt on the day that she looked across the nursery and saw Treasure standing by the lettuce garden.

Her face was shaded by a broad-brimmed raffia hat. Over her breasts she wore a narrow, white bandeau and beneath her great, swollen stomach, a flowing cheesecloth skirt. All of the rest of her was lightly bronzed flesh and deep golden hair that fell in a single thick plait down her spine. Over the crook of her elbow was a basket. In the basket was one of the Christmas lilies which Meg had planted out months ago in lovely glazed ceramic pots. Meg obscured herself, stepping sideways behind a screen threaded with calligraphic fronds of clematis. Still, she had a clear view of Treasure as she strolled around the slightly raked display garden with its sloping, russet-green tapestry of leaves. It was one of the romaine varieties that Treasure reached for, plucking a young, pale green leaf from its heart. And as Meg watched, feeling unaccountably violated, she ate it.

❦

'Probably she didn't think of it as stealing,' Cathie said.

It was just after New Year by the time Meg had the opportunity to report back on the incident at the nursery and this time the café table had to accommodate Jen's acid yellow pram as well as Cathie's lime green one. Jen fiddled at the rim of her shirt with her baby's tiny mouth and a nipple.

'Well, what else would you call it?' Meg said.

Meg remembered something that happened to her, when she was quite young, in the vegetable section of the supermarket. In those days there were scales—the ones with deep silver bowls and old-fashioned red-needled dials—hanging near the apples and pears so that customers could weigh their purchases. Meg's mother had been busy looking at her list when Meg had absent-mindedly plucked a plump green grape, popped it into her mouth, and felt a pinch on her upper arm. It hurt. The perpetrator was a woman and she was bending down to Meg's height wagging a finger in censure. She wore the supermarket's cotton drill uniform and a badge upon her chest, but the most vivid thing in Meg's memory was the way her bright lipstick bled into all the lines of her little arsehole of a mouth. It turned out to be a highly effective pinch. Meg was permanently put off theft. And grapes.

'You know what they say about lettuce, though,' Cathie said.

But Meg had no idea what they said about lettuce.

'You know: "Lettuce is a free food",' Cathie explained.

'Says who?' Meg asked.

'Diet books,' said Cathie. 'When you're dieting, lettuce and spinach are free. You can have as much as you want.'

'No calories,' said Jen. 'No consequences.'

⁂

Meg began to labour on a Sunday morning in mid-January and, within an hour of the serious onset of contractions, her inner sunflower had been torn out of the ground with cyclonic force. After a further half hour of clenching and wrenching and squeezing, she was prepared to admit that she had come in underprepared, that she had failed to grasp that pain could go up so far on the scale. But these were admissions of surpassing uselessness. There was nothing she could do, now, except hope to survive.

Jackson Alexander Campbell—Jack for everyday—was born in the afternoon. The pain had been of tectonic magnitude, but then came the equal and opposite reaction, a swamping tide of passion for the child in her arms, for the man whose face was echoed so cleverly in the angle of the chin and the shape of the nose.

'Hey, good work, Fat Guts,' said Justin, although his voice was so tender that, had Meg chosen, she could easily have heard him differently.

That evening, Meg's mother came to the hospital to meet her grandson.

'Did you . . . ?' Meg began.

Meg was tired and weepy by now and uncertain she could continue, and yet there was something she had to know. 'Mum, did you feel this? Did you . . . love me this much?'

Meg looked closely at her mother, and at the unkindnesses done to her face by the years of trying to hold it all perfectly together. The scoldings, the crossness, the indignation: they all showed. But, even so, they were not up to the task of hiding her wistfulness.

'Hold on to that feeling, Meggie,' her mother said. 'Because it has to last you for a very, very long time.'

✷

That night, Meg slept only a little. The sheets on the hospital bed were over-starched and heavy, and the room was faintly lit from the green glow of tiny bulbs on the light sockets and call buttons. Meg was aware of pain—in her lower back, in her pelvis, in the torn but stitched-up skin of her vulva—and she could smell the strong animal scent of afterbirth coming from the pad wedged between her thighs. This night was the beginning of her new way of listening. In the semi-darkness, in the gaps between Justin's snores, she sent her senses out into the room in search of the sighing sounds of a baby breathing, while in the next room, another woman laboured.

Early the next day Justin went off to work. Meg didn't mind. She spent the morning in bed with Jack—wearing nothing but his tiny nappy—lying on her bare chest. Through her half-open door she saw the rolling stacks of breakfast trays come and go, caught glimpses of the doctors with their clipboards, watched the blue-shirted midwives towing their blood pressure machines from room to room. Late in the morning, there was animated talking at the reception desk that was just a short distance down the hallway from Meg's room, but listen as she might in her new acute fashion, Meg could not work out what it was all about. The lunch trays came and went, and still there was low talking in the corridor. It was generating a low-frequency hum of wrongness, of drama. Meg held her healthy baby tight to her chest and wondered if there had been a stillbirth.

'A baby's been left,' explained a midwife who came in to see to Meg.

'Left?'

'The mother didn't want it,' the midwife said with a sniff of contempt. 'It's thrown us all a bit. They get this sort of thing quite often over at the public hospital, but we're not really used to it here.'

Meg wanted to wash and that was a good enough reason to haul herself painfully out of bed. She would take Jack to the nursery and ask the midwives there to watch him for half an hour while she showered. Meg's mother had told her how, back in her day, the babies spent the better part of their time with the staff in the Roseneath nursery so that the mothers might recuperate after the birth, but Meg was unsure which was pathetic and which was not: these modern mothers wanting their babies in their rooms with them all the day and night, or those old-fashioned mothers who'd been allowed to rest.

Meg wheeled Jack in his plastic crib to the nursery. Only one of the cribs there was occupied. Two midwives stood beside it. According to their badges they were called Cyn and Sue, and Meg could tell from the way they dropped their voices in response to her presence that they knew they ought to be discreet. The baby in the crib was quite small compared with Jack. She slept upon her back, elbows bent, tiny fists framing her petite face, and the sight of her Cupid's bow lips and of the fine curlicues of damp, dark-gold hair against her skull was more than just the last piece of Meg's jigsaw puzzle. It was the key to a picture Meg had been looking at upside down, or slantwise, or in some other wrong way.

'She's beautiful,' Meg offered, and it was enough for the midwives to decide that the mother had forfeited all right to discretion.

Cyn said, 'The mother held her for a minute, had a good look at her, then just passed her back to Sue and said, "You can take her away now, thank you."'

'I've seen it happen that mothers don't want to hold their babies right away,' Sue said. 'So I took the baby to the nursery and we looked after her here for a few hours to let Mum sleep off the birth. But, next thing you know, she's up and packed her suitcase—you know, one of those little air-hostessy numbers—and checked herself out. Said she wasn't taking the baby and if there were any forms to sign we could just send them on.'

The baby girl opened her newborn-blue eyes and made a thin cry.

'I'll fix her some formula,' said Cyn. 'Poor wee thing.'

'Does she have a name?' Meg asked.

'No name,' Sue said.

'We should give her one,' said Cyn.

Meg reached out and touched the baby's cheek with one of her irretrievably dirt-stained gardener's fingers.

'You could call her Lettuce,' Meg said.

'Lettuce?'

'Why Lettuce?'

Because lettuce is a free food, Meg thought, although she only shrugged.

'Just cos,' said a male obstetrician, who was at the nursery desk making notes on a patient's chart, and who hadn't appeared to be listening.

'You're terrible,' said Cyn.

'I think it suits her, actually,' said Sue.

The baby girl wore a pale green gro-suit out of the nursery's emergency clothing stash and under the bright hospital lights it was casting a tint up under her chin the way a buttercup does on a sunny day.

'Lettuce she is then,' said Sue, and she wrote it in upper-case letters on the small square of whiteboard above the crib.

ॐ

In the evenings of all the years in which her boys were growing up, it was Meg's habit to step outside just before dinner into the kitchen garden with a pair of snips and the big red enamel colander. She would slide the heavy glass doors closed on the noise and demands inside, and—for just a few moments—be among her plants. The beds were rimmed with nicely greyed timber sleepers and Meg liked the way there was no particular order to the plantings of nasturtium, rosemary, chives, sweetpea and lettuce. In the evening cool, while harvesting herbs and salad leaves, she would often think of little Lettuce's face, and wonder whatever became of her.

Sometimes Meg thought of Treasure, too. That was usually in the supermarket. It was the mirrors that did it, the ones at the back of the cabinets that were there to enhance the apparent abundance of the fruits and the vegetables, to multiply the fish fillets on their ice beds and to pick up the appetising sheen on the roast chooks. Meg would be bagging a parsnip when she'd look up and catch sight of herself, face bare of lipstick or mascara, hair shoved back in a rough ponytail, snot trails on the shoulder of her nursery vest. And those other mirrors: women all around with nappy boxes taking up three quarters of their trolley space, scouring the backs of packets for *may contain traces of nuts*, yelling 'Put that back, please', 'No running, please', 'Please stop yanking on the trolley'. It was something that Meg had not known until she had children, how easily *please* can be made to stand in for *for fuck's sake*.

Of course, Treasure wouldn't have to do any of this. Nothing would force her to trudge the biscuit aisle the way Meg did, with Jack hanging off the side of the trolley and Will still small enough, just, to sit on the fold-out seat shoving fat handfuls of sultanas into his endlessly open mouth. Each week Meg threw into her trolley two big bags full of small packs of Tiny Teddies, even though *Choice* magazine once named them as the worst of a bad bunch of kiddy snacks, and even though the amount of packaging this purchase entailed was a crime.

Small packs of Tiny Teddies were currency with which you could buy silence in five-minute grabs. Meg pushed her trolley past the Venetians, the Kingstons and the Caramel Crowns. The Orange Slices reminded her that some people could get away with it, but a quick glance at her girth in the gratuitously placed mirror on the pillar in the middle of the aisle told her, as if she didn't already know, that she was not one of them.

At Meg's local supermarket, the magazine aisle was also the toy aisle, so while the boys ogled the Matchbox cars and the action figures, Meg could linger for a moment. She never so much as touched the gossip magazines which she knew to be more full of crap and worse for you than Tim Tams, but she saw, without exactly reading, their headlines. Always there was a *baby bump* and an *amazing post-baby body* and *twins!* and a *miracle conception*. She hankered after a *Gourmet Traveller* or even a *Better Homes and Gardens*, but they weren't on the list.

Once, and only ever once, Meg caught a glimpse of Treasure. Meg was driving through the city and had stopped at some traffic lights, and there she was, sitting on a high stool at the bench seat in the window of a café. Visible beneath the bench was the soft leather of a pair of tan high-heeled boots. Above it were dark blonde curls falling onto the frilled collar of a houndstooth trench coat. Meg could easily imagine how, in the middle, the belt of the coat would cinch a perfectly retracted waist. But it wasn't any of those things that made Meg turn the radio news up louder and clutch the steering wheel harder. It was the solitary coffee and the leisurely newspaper spread out upon the countertop.

'Mummy!' Jack bellowed from the backseat. 'Mu-u-um. Mum!'

Meg ignored him, even though she knew that in so doing she was probably cauterising yet another square millimetre of a heart whose hardness she would one day grieve.

'Mummamummamummamummamumma,' babbled Will, sitting next to him.

She imagined her future self reaching back through time to slap her own cheek and say, "Turn around and speak to your sons", but even by way of this trick she could conjure up nothing in her heart to share.

'Mum!' yelled Jack. 'Muuuuuuuuuuuuuuuuuuuum!'

'Mummamummamumma!'

'Why you cry, Mummy?' asked Jack.

'Why you *cry*, Mummy? Talk to me, Mummy! Mummy! MUMMY!'

cottage

The man and the woman together made the decision to walk their children into the woods, just as together they made the children. So why does she always get the blame?

WHEN HENRY BEGAN childcare he developed the habit—in the mornings while his mother Nina was dressing—of filling his pockets with such small items as he could find about the house. Then, when it was time to leave, Nina, already buttoned into her coat, would kneel down on the threshold to divest him of his treasures.

There was a morning when she unpocketed a miniature Batmobile, three marbles, a biro and four toy soldiers, along with some other, less expected items: a safety pin, a thumb drive, a plectrum and a tampon. Nina blushed at the thought as she shoved the tampon in her coat pocket, although not fast enough.

'What's that thing, Mummy?'

But it was 7.45 and there wasn't time. Not even for obfuscation.

'Is there anything else?'

Henry widened his pale eyes, shook his head solemnly, and Nina sighed.

'There's a rule, remember? No home toys allowed.'

Nina was telling the truth about this.

'But Charlie brings home toys. And Hazel.'

Henry, too, was telling the truth. It irked Nina that other parents didn't follow the rules.

It wasn't only the pockets of his clothes that she had to search—the deep side-pockets of his parka, all five pockets of his overalls and the easy-to-forget knitted pockets on each end of his scarf—but all the zippered nooks of his bag, too. In these he had squirreled a squash ball, a tea-light candle, a spoon, a cotton reel, a padlock, some nail clippers. Also the thimble-sized bucket from his pirate ship set. Nina made a sad face.

'How would you feel if you lost this at school?'

It wasn't school of course—he had only just turned two. The word was supposed to make him feel older and her less guilty.

'Please?' Henry asked, reaching out again for the toy bucket. 'I bring it back. I promise.'

But you *won't*, but you *don't*, but you *just can't be expected to*, Nina whined to herself as she got to her feet. Henry looked mournfully at his robbed cache, now just a jumble of junk on the kitchen table.

What were Henry's plans? Might things have turned out differently, Nina now wonders, had she not daily emptied out his pockets before walking him to the car and driving a disorienting pattern of lefts and rights to the other side of the city, to the place where she would leave him? If only she had left herself a trail in moon-bright pebbles, or white-bread crumbs, she might have been able to find her way back through the months and weeks to find out.

Nina had never imagined that Henry would go to childcare. She had never wanted any child of hers in one of those places. She disliked them the way she disliked old people's homes, those other dumping grounds for the incontinent and inconvenient. Before Henry was even conceived, she had told Lucas how she felt. He had said he understood, and they had made a deal. Nina would stay at home and care for their child and Lucas would work to support them.

Theirs was an old-fashioned arrangement and very strange to Nina's friends. Even those who didn't say 'But, what about your career?', or 'How are you going to afford it?', or 'Won't you be bored witless?' were thinking it. Nina could tell by the looks on their faces, just as she could see the traces of unspoken offence she had caused them with her decision and its implications. She tried self-deprecation: 'But you're so amazing! If *I* tried to work and raise a baby at the same time, I'd just end up doing both things badly.' But she was never quite sure how convincing she was. She supposed the truth was all over her face, too.

Genevieve was the only friend with whom Nina felt she could be honest. Genevieve had made a pragmatic marriage to an older man who adored both her and his own very successful pursuit of riches. She didn't need to work, but did so anyway in order to avoid her marriage becoming—as she called it—transactional.

Genevieve was tall and androgynously slim with close-cropped hair and she made Nina feel small and voluptuous by comparison, although in isolation she wasn't really either. Genevieve had large, strange eyes with pupils of normal size but vast expanses of white surrounding them. Her gaze could be fearsomely intense. Nina partly disliked the no-holds-barred conversations she had with Genevieve, however she suspected they were good for her. In this friendship there were periods of silence while Nina sulked, but once she was over the latest insult or slight, she would pick up the phone and pretend nothing had ever happened.

'So you think full-time mothers do a better job then, do you?' Genevieve said, the touch of South African in her accent coming to the fore as it often did when she was in the interrogative mode.

She and Nina were sitting across from each other at the breakfast bar in Genevieve's kitchen. Nina was near to full term.

'Well, yes I do,' Nina confessed.

'I can tell you for certain that I'm a better mother because I'm away from them a bit each week.'

Nina was listening, but also watching Genevieve's three-year-old daughter tiptoeing in with the intention of swiping a fingerful of butter from the open dish on the bar. Nina couldn't help it—she was pregnant and watching other people's children carefully, as if for clues. Her gaze betrayed little Phoebe's whereabouts.

'If I were with them all the time, I think I'd . . . *eat them all up!*' Genevieve made her eyes yet more terrifying, and Phoebe ran away, squealing joyfully.

'She's gorgeous,' Nina said.

'Yar. Childcare two days a week since she was one and no scars at all.'

'I'm sorry, Gen. We're not going to agree on this one.'

'Your baby won't ever thank you for it, you know, Nina. And you can't get an A+ for this—it isn't school.'

True, Nina was accustomed to reward for effort. She had worked for fifteen years in a sequence of high-pressure jobs in current affairs radio, and everyone said she was a brilliant producer. But she was longing for a change, even if it meant returning to the modest, inexpensive way of life she remembered, almost fondly now, from her student days. She planned to buy second-hand clothes for herself and the baby, take a Thermos of coffee to the park instead of going to cafés, cook at home rather than eat out, save on petrol by fitting a baby seat to the bicycle; maybe even sell her car and get by with only Lucas's. She and the baby would entertain themselves by going to the museum and the library; they would walk on the foreshore and spend slow afternoons with their hands in the earth of their own backyard. And she'd make it worth

Lucas's while. She'd be relaxed and happy. And when he got home in the evenings, she'd have his dinner ready.

For his part, Lucas—who ran his own sound engineering business—agreed that he would work longer hours if necessary, and take on the kind of corporate work that he normally considered a waste of his talent. He accepted that he'd have to put his songwriting on hold for a while, take a break from the band. Lucas said that up until the kid was three ought to be long enough but Nina insisted on school age, and Lucas said okay, so long as Nina promised not to push for a second child. They shook on it.

There were so many ways in which it went wrong for them. The first casualty was dinner, which was never—not once, not ever—on the table when Lucas got home from work. Henry was a colicky baby and his management, especially in the early days, involved complicated sequences of feeding, swaddling, patting, rocking and swinging. Various medications were prescribed to combat his reflux, but each came with side effects that had their separate ways of preventing Henry from sleeping for longer than forty minutes at a stretch.

Nina's love for Henry was fierce, of course. That was a given, but from the very beginning it was also inflected with a fear born of her suspicion that she needed him more than he needed her, and that he had—or at least would grow to have—the capacity to reject her in the most primal and hurtful of ways. She sensed this in the way he fed: fitfully, frequently, taking tiny sips of breastmilk and then pursing his little mouth, straining away with all the strength he had in his dandelion-stalk of a neck. Once or twice Nina googled how early you could tell if your child was a sociopath, then erased her search history in shame.

Henry was thin. He was prone to mysterious skin rashes and unexplained vomiting. He didn't show up as allergic to anything in particular; he just seemed determined not to thrive. When the time came to add solid food to his diet, Nina spent hours at the food processor, trying out different combinations. Banana and raspberry. Spinach and sweet potato. Pumpkin, carrot and orange. Mango and pear. Blueberry and ricotta. She would try to tempt Henry with these mixtures, sometimes getting frustrated and forcing the food in by levering down his lower jaw with the bottom of the spoon, but even if she got a small quantity past his lips and teeth, he would only spit it out again. The bibs Nina left soaking in the laundry buckets were stained every colour of the fruit and vegetable rainbow.

Each week, Nina took Henry to the child health clinic to be weighed. On a good week he gained a few grams, but, even so, he was struggling to keep up with the chart's lowest percentile. About the only thing he liked were Milk Arrowroot biscuits soaked in sugared milk, so Nina lowered her standards and fed them to him. Still, his growth was painfully slow, and when Nina pinched his little arms and legs they felt as thin and fragile as chicken bones.

Nina fretted over Henry so much that her hair—her beautiful hair that was long and thick, the darkest of reds—began to fall out in handfuls. When it later came back, it was mottled with white in splotches above one eyebrow and behind both ears. Lucas did all that he could to help. He told Nina as little as possible about his company's failing finances, and, so that she might capitulate for a few hours to her exhaustion, he would drive the streets by night, tracing Tetris patterns around the city blocks in his thrumming Valiant station wagon, while Henry griped and bawled from the capsule in the back seat. Sometimes when Lucas got sick of the noise he moved the capsule to the passenger side of the Val's broad bench seat and drove with his right hand while Henry slurped on the pinkie of his left.

When Henry turned one, he and Nina were yet to visit the library, or the museum. There had been no time to fit the bicycle seat, let alone put Nina's car on the market. The earth in the garden was cracked and lifeless, the whereabouts of the Thermos unknown. The reflux had settled, but Henry had become accustomed to days on Nina's hip and nights in Nina and Lucas's bed. Nina and Lucas rarely had sex anymore and, if they did, it was of the 'help yourself' variety where Nina would remain half-asleep in the dark, while Lucas as quietly as possible did whatever he needed to do. It wasn't that Nina believed the old wives' tale about the contraceptive powers of frequent breastfeeding, nor did she forget to take the Pill one day, or even two in a row. It was only that she more or less forgot that there was such a thing as contraception or that she might need it.

'I'm pregnant,' she told Lucas, when Henry was just over a year old.

'That wasn't the deal,' he said.

'The deal was that I wouldn't ask for another baby. And I didn't.'

'I suppose it's too late.'

'I hope you're not suggesting what I think you're suggesting.'

'I thought you were on the Pill.'

'Thought, but didn't ask. Excuse me, what year is this?'

So Gracie was born—easy little Gracie, who ate and slept and smiled and loved Nina effortlessly in all the ways Nina had expected Henry to, and Nina was grateful, as well as guilty for foisting upon Henry a little sister who was so clearly everything he was not. And Lucas read all the pamphlets about getting the snip, and everything that was already wrong became worse, and if Lucas thought that he was being starved of Nina's undivided attention when they had only Henry, he soon learned that the universe had a whole other outer rim for him to inhabit. But he did get his wife's attention, all of it, one night when Gracie was just eight weeks old and Henry almost two.

Once the children were in bed he sat down with Nina and told her that the business was now insolvent and that their bank's willingness to extend the mortgage on their home had reached its limit. A friend had offered him an entry-level job at a large sound company but the pay was meagre, only enough to service the now-inflated mortgage repayments. She stared at him.

Lucas sat forward on the couch, his buttocks barely on the seat, his hands folded penitently together between his knees. She stared at the sinewy lengths of his calves and of his forearms, at the entire pale, freckled stretch of him. On a stage, with his chest bare and a shirt tangled around those hips, he was sexy in a rangy sort of way, but here and now he seemed to her only flimsy and vulnerable, as well as adolescent in an infuriating way that provoked sympathy he didn't deserve. He'd looked much like this, and with this same shamed, defeated, defiant look on his face, six years ago when his boutique record booth had failed and they'd been unable to repay the start-up money loaned to them by Nina's father. And again when he'd sat on the same couch—wearing those same brown leather sandals, now Nina comes to think of it—confessing to her that he had gambled away on the internet the nest egg—not huge, but not inconsiderable either—left to him by his mother.

When Nina first saw Lucas, she was twenty years old and mistook his ungainly hopelessness for a sign that female interest in him would be limited, even exclusive, perhaps, to her. But she soon discovered that his dope-sleepy eyes and the careless harmonics picked out on a guitar perched on a speckled knee had actually quite a broad appeal. Lucas's desirability to other women, and to Janey Cooper in particular, only intensified Nina's attraction to him. While bubbly little Janey danced for him, front and centre at every gig, Nina had her own methods. She spent months of Friday and Saturday nights numbing her buttocks on bar stools and rejecting Lucas's advances with just the perfect measures of come-hitherishness and disdain. At last she saw off her competition and had Lucas humming 'Nina, Pretty Ballerina' instead of 'Lady Jane' into the back-up mike between songs.

That she had fought to win something she was no longer sure she should ever have wanted was not an easy admission to make, and it was only getting harder with every passing year. It wasn't only the obvious things—marriage, Henry, Gracie—that had dug her in so deep, but also the many times she excused him, forgave him, apologised for him. Throwing good money after bad, her father would have said. Had said, although he was talking about actual cash and not the type of investment Nina had made.

'We'll have to sell the house,' Nina said.

The house. They had bought it as a down-at-heel workers' cottage, left by generations of landlords and student tenants to flake and peel and rot on a small, rhomboid-shaped block on the fringe of the city. Nina and Lucas had gussied up the street frontage and borrowed money to build a new section out the back: a rustic timber and glass atrium that snared the sun and had a view over the last shrub-shrouded reach of the rivulet before the watercourse went underground to sieve itself through the foundations of the city and seep out to sea. There was barely an inch of the house, inside or out, that Nina and Lucas hadn't sanded or polished or painted, but now Nina felt her love for the place slip off like a too-big glove. It took only a moment for her to imagine herself happy in a rental in the outer suburbs, to envision how they would cover the awful wallpaper with art and repaint the kitchen cupboards and find local parks where the kids could play on the swings. But it wasn't that simple, Lucas told her: even if they sold the house, and for a good price, they would still have a sizeable debt, yet nowhere to live. Rent plus debt and they'd be no better off.

Nina thought of Jane Carslake, who used to be Janey Cooper, but was now married to an orthopaedic surgeon and put her kids in childcare half a day a week, and that was only so she could go to the gym and keep her nails and hair in order. Even as she had this thought, Nina was ashamed for having it, as well as amazed by the capacity of financial reality to bring her shallows up out of her depths.

'I did tell you each time I made a redraw,' he said.

'But you didn't tell me it was serious.'

'It turns out that it is.'

Nina was quiet and careful, the way she always was when handling Lucas's ego. It was almost like a pet to her, a creature she had milk-fed and hand-reared, and her abiding instinct was to shelter it. On the other occasions they had found themselves here—he on the couch, she sitting on one of the dining chairs nursing her fallen heart in her lap—she had said that it didn't really matter, that accidents happened, that everything would be alright, that somehow they would work through it, together. Not this time. When at last she spoke, she kept her voice small, as if this might prevent it from betraying the dimensions of her unsurprised disappointment.

'We had a deal.'

'You? *You* want to bring up the deal?'

'This is my only chance, the only one I will ever have, to be a mother and do it properly. You promised.'

Nina already knew what it was that Lucas expected her to do, and it was clear to her that she was going to have to do it. And yet it seemed to her important, in this instance, that he should be the one to say it out loud.

'So, what are we going to do about it?' she asked.

'Other people do it,' he said.

'Do what, Lucas?'

The rolling of the eyes was teenage, incendiary.

'Do what, Lucas?'

'Oh, come on. You know.'

'Other people fuck their dogs. Is that what you mean?'

And so, against Nina's better judgement, they fought. They each dredged up the most forbidden of their ammunition out of deep storage. They said things they meant, and things they didn't mean; Lucas shouting and swearing, Nina hissing and pointing at the door beyond which their children lay sleeping, until at last, she lost control.

'Fine, then,' she yelled. 'I'll go back to work and we'll just dump our children in some awful fucking overcrowded child-care centre so they can get every cold and flu and rash known to humankind and be raised by doe-eyed, semi-educated, underpaid morons instead of by their own parents.'

There came a sound from beyond the door. Perhaps a small hip knocking against a wall, perhaps a half-full bottle of milk falling onto the carpet.

'Oh, Jesus,' Nina said.

Lucas got to the door first. And there stood Henry in the centre of the hallway runner, pear-shaped in his onesie pyjamas, his fair hair riled with static. A corner of his sky-blue sucky blanket was balled into his mouth.

'It's alright, mate,' Lucas said. 'Mummy and I were just . . .'

In Henry's terrified eyes Nina saw the car smash, the five-storey fall, the irreversible, the incurable. Even as she felt her heart plunge into a place where it was already too late, the damage done, her mind leapt forward into the fixing of it.

'Mummy's here, Mummy's here,' Nina said, pushing past Lucas and scooping Henry, blanket and all, into her arms. She took him to his room, small and softly night-lit, and shut the door behind them. Nina held him tight within the four close walls that were painted in a shade of greenish blue that she had chosen when he had been still in her belly. She had hung that block-mounted poster of the cover of *The Little Prince* above his bed when the exact shape and form of Henry had been still a dream to her.

'Where you taking us? Mumma?'

'Nowhere, Henry. Nowhere.'

Beneath the rocket ship she had suspended from the celestial ceiling whose constellations she had set out, one star and moon and comet at a time, she held as much of him as she could, folding both of his arms against her breast, cradling his skull with outspread fingers, nuzzling her nose into his hair.

'Who . . . who . . . is going to look after to us?' he asked.

Look after to us. It was a formulation she hadn't been able to correct.

'I will, darling,' she said, her mouth on her son's sweet cheek. 'I will.'

⌘

It was called The Cottage, although it was no more a cottage than it was a school. It was a low, brick, purpose-built centre and the path to its front door was an avenue of plaster toad-stools with plaster hedgehogs, squirrels and rabbits nesting cutely around their bases. In the mornings Nina struggled up that path with Henry's hand in hers and Gracie on one hip, both children's bags slung awkwardly over her shoulders. She had to turn sideways to allow for the mothers coming the other way. Nina didn't mind the tight-lipped ones, the ones who drew their cardigans in tight as the double-glazed doors sealed behind them, shutting off the sound of a child's wailing. To those ones, Nina would offer a weak, watery smile, knowing as well as they that there was nothing helpful to be said or done.

It was the other mothers she disliked, the ones with older, well-adjusted children in the big preschool rooms at the end of the corridor. Those mothers almost skipped down the path on their way to work and Nina knew they talked about her, and about poor little Gracie, only three months old and in care five days a week. She never heard them, but she saw the way they looked at her, and she knew. She would have talked about herself.

Henry was quiet on the path. He didn't baulk, or protest. Not then. He would walk with one hand in Nina's and the other thrust into one of his deep, emptied pockets, calm and self-contained, as if preparing himself. He was docile in Gracie's room where the younger babies lay on bunny rugs on the carpet and the older ones pulled themselves up to their feet and tottered around the play equipment, falling from time to time back down onto their nappy-fat bottoms. It was almost too easy to leave Gracie, who was pleased to see everyone and too young to know that it was not normal to spend all day with strangers. Nina wrote out labels for bottles of expressed breastmilk, set out Gracie's day's worth of nappies, hung her little knitted hat on her own special peg.

Nina did not hurry through the leaving of Gracie, but she always made sure there would be enough time to linger in

Henry's room and help him do puzzles, or make snails from the centre's bright blue and green and yellow play dough. It gave her time to observe and amass evidence: that unattended child with its nappy loose and brown juice leaking down its leg, the little girl who gave a horror movie shriek as a boy leant in gleefully to fasten his mouth around her forearm, leaving behind a full imprint of his milk teeth. Nina watched the children in the corner with the toy cooker and the timber pots playing at a game they called 'Mums and Dads' in which one child would lie on the floor making baby cry noises, while two others gave it a good scolding. After a time they would all swap around.

Henry's primary carer was Beverly. She was young for a grandmother, with hectic platinum hair and ruby-rimmed glasses that hung around her neck on a lanyard strung with bright baubles. She had the voice of a reformed smoker, sweet but still slightly phlegmy, and her conversations with Nina were seamlessly interspersed with 'Not them ones, George' and 'Can we have a bit of shush please, Lucinda?' and 'Hazel, no hat, no play, my little cherub'. Every day Beverly wore the centre's uniform of navy pants and a navy polo shirt with a red and white toadstool logo and *The Cottage* embroidered on the pocket, but she wore the shirt unbuttoned and this allowed a glimpse of the Kiss tattoo inked in fading red, blue and black on the crepe-textured skin to one side of her cleavage.

'You're a big fan, then?' Nina said, gesturing to her own décolletage.

'Love 'em,' Beverly confirmed and, although her tone was perfectly polite, Nina could tell the conversation was already at an end.

One morning Nina saw Beverly showing a photograph of her infant granddaughter to a colleague. Beverly wished she could afford not to work full-time—Nina heard her say—so she could help her daughter out more. Together the women turned back to the photo, smiling and cooing, but when Nina said, 'Oh, let me see', Beverly dutifully passed her the photograph while carrying on the conversation with her colleague without pause.

Nina could tell that Beverly was neither flattered nor intrigued by Nina's interest in her, and Nina was irritated and vaguely hurt by the fact that she didn't have, or feel she had, more purchase over Beverly. Although theirs was a user pays arrangement—transactional, as Genevieve would say—Nina couldn't shake either the sense that she was indebted to Beverly, or the suspicion that Beverly despised her. And not just Nina, but all of them: all the working mothers with their pretty shoes and swishy coats who left their lost little children in her care.

Nina felt she was entitled to know at least something about the woman who was caring for her son, but Beverly refused to open up; and she did so in a way that let Nina know Beverly thought she was asking for something she had not paid for and had no right to expect. Charm didn't help Nina in her dealings with Beverly. Nina sensed that Beverly came from a place that Nina had never been to—somewhere harder and more honest, where charm was as useful as leftover coins from a foreign country.

Beverly gave Nina advice on saying goodbye. 'All you say is "I'm going to work now, Henry". Nothing else. Then you hand him to me and off you go. And no looking back.'

Despite Nina's best efforts to remain calm and inscrutable, it always happened a few minutes before leaving time that she would feel the guilty prickle of adrenalin in the backs of her hands, and Henry would sense that his time was approaching. A slick of wetness would appear across the surface of his eyes, and his lower lip would begin to wobble.

'I come with you to work, Mummy? I be good,' he would say.

Normally, Nina would enter into a long explanation, but here at the centre, Beverly would be watching.

'I'm going to work now, Henry,' she would say. 'I love you.'

Beverly would give Nina a stern little look, hold out her arms to the child.

'Come on, Henry. You and me'll go feed the chooky girls, hey?'

To begin with, there would be discernable words: *no* and *Mummy* and *please*. By the time Nina reached the door these would have scrambled into incoherence, although there was no mistaking the meaning of the piercing screams, the way he would punch and kick at Beverly, who held his thrashing little body fast in her tuckshop lady arms. Nina would feel her child's distress sluice through her, sending a wash of ice up under her hair and down the backs of her legs. She would hear him all the way down the corridor and onto the path, when the door would close behind her, although it didn't really stop then. His crying echoed within her all the way to the car, all the way to work through the morning-choked streets, stowing away in the curling corridors of her ears even as she entered the station building.

This was a place adapted for the transmission and protection of sound: its doors heavy, its walls padded and ceilings furred. Even the air here had a different quality: thin, as if depleted of some crucial element so that sound might speed through it just a little quicker. Once, Nina had been used to breathing this air, had even thrived on it. But now each time she arrived at work, she felt instantly tired, lethargic and foggy, as if she had altitude sickness. She could see that the station manager was regretting his decision to dismiss a probationary graduate in order to fit her back into the team. And her presenter—an ambitious younger man, stopping off in radio by way of transit to television—did little to hide his disappointment at being landed with a lemon.

Nina found it hard to concentrate. There were days when the whiteboard seemed larger than previously and the slots she must fill with controversy and chatter more numerous. She was so distracted that she would dial a number and set someone's phone to ringing, only to slam the receiver down in a rush of panic at realising she had forgotten in the space of a moment both whom she was calling and why. There were too many occasions when the presenter on the other side of the soundproof glass had to struggle for banalities to fill the passing seconds as Nina's trembling hands hovered over the blinking lights and dials of the control panel, all the labels and codes suddenly stripped of meaning. While the show was to air, there was no time for the bathroom and yet Nina would find herself there, holding those shuddering hands under the cold tap and trying not to look at herself in the mirror. This was the mirror in which she had observed herself in those early days of her pregnancy with Henry, looking for signs. In the same mirror she had later watched her shape morphing day by day. Now it showed the splashes of white in her hair that looked not so much the result of mishap, but only further evidence of disorganisation and failure.

There were days, though, when the work succeeded in seducing her into the worlds of opinion and talkback, dragging her out into the tired kitchens of the country's lonely nutcases and pedants. On these days she would slip away from who she was, all the way out to the end of her leash, which would at last snap tight and jerk her heart right up into her throat. *Oh, God, the children! The children! Where are the children?*

'You do know that Henry is completely fine, though,' Genevieve counselled. 'You've seen other children do it, right? Carry on like pork chops until their parents are out of sight and then, suddenly, they're completely fine.'

But Nina was far from certain that this was true for Henry. At home on the weekends, he became nervous each time

Nina picked up her car keys, and a couple of times when he woke from an afternoon sleep while Nina was out at the clothesline, he had become convinced that he had been left alone in the house. When Nina returned with the washing basket she found him walking through the house screwing his sucky blanket into a twist as he cried, hysterical with fear. There were evenings when she would arrive at the centre to find him with his eyes red and puffy, his breathing jagged.

'Is he like this all day?' Nina asked Beverly.

'He's a little down sometimes,' Beverly said.

This was understatement, Nina knew. She also knew as well as Beverly did that speaking the whole truth changed nothing about Henry's situation.

'Shouldn't you call me, if he's distressed?' Nina wanted to ask more forcefully than, in the end, she felt able to. Beggars can't be choosers.

'He'll settle in. They all do, eventually.'

But although the weeks passed, Henry and Nina's daily separations became no easier. It seemed not to matter that precisely the same thing happened five days out of every seven: it was clear that each time Nina passed Henry into Beverly's arms and turned her back, the little boy felt the shock of her betrayal afresh.

Genevieve tried hard to console Nina. 'You've got to admit there's something gratifying about how pleased they are to see you at the end of the day.'

Nina knew what Genevieve was talking about. Mothers

at day's end were minor celebrities, and in that dismal hour between five and six, when most of the children had already been collected and the carers were tired and trying to set out the next day's paint pots and felt pictures and box work, one or two children would hover about the door in the capacity of forward scouts, to watch for them.

'That's Charlie's mummy.'

'No, tisn't.'

'Yes, tis.'

'Charlie's mummy has tall shoes. That's Lucinda's mummy.'

'Lucinda! Lucinda! Your mummy's here!'

And Lucinda would appear with her wild hair and paint-smeared clothes and run at her mother's legs fit to break them. It was only Henry's second week in care when he gave up responding to the sentries' announcements. He no longer came running—relieved and rescued—to Nina's open arms. Instead, Nina would have to go looking for him. She might find him among the cushions in the library corner, or squatting down, alone, in a corner of the small Colorbond shed in which the tricycles were kept. One evening she found him crouching low on the far side of the chicken pen, in a narrow space between the wire and a paling fence. The big tawny birds had only recently been given a reprieve from a battery farm; they were still apt to peck up pebbles and sticks in their blunt clipped-away beaks. Henry watched them sadly, his body juddering with the occasional weary sob.

'Why don't you have Lucas take him to childcare some

days?' Genevieve said. 'Let your bloody husband take his fair share of it. He wanted to become a father.'

Genevieve had a way of making these things sound so obvious.

'I don't think that's a good idea.'

'Why not? Henry might be easier for his dad.'

'No,' said Nina. The suggestion made her feel angry and panicked.

Already such a large part of Henry's day was lost to her. Some nights after childcare, when she lifted Henry into the bathtub, there were marks on his body that he could not explain. They were only small scratches and bruises, just the normal stuff of childhood, but once upon a time she would have known how the tricycle fell over and where on the asphalt of the park Henry had left the scrapings of his knee. Now these marks were the story of his day apart from her. They were all that was left of a stretch of hours that he could not describe, and that remained, to Nina, a blank.

On weekdays, Nina was nothing more than the person who woke and fed and dressed Henry in the morning, and who fed and undressed and put Henry to bed at night. Meanwhile, in the intervening hours, other women were filling his mind. Nina had good intentions of making up for it on Saturdays and Sundays with cooking and nature walks and doing puzzles on the living room floor, but somehow the weekends filled themselves with the chores required to sustain the working week. It was often the best she could do, as she folded the endless piles of washing, to have Henry leaf through an alphabet book beside her.

'What letter is that one, Henry? You know that one,' Nina said.

'Haitch,' said Henry,

'Excuse me?'

'Haitch. Haitch for Henry.'

'You mean "aitch",' Nina said.

'No, it's "haitch",' Henry said. 'Bevelly told me. At school.'

Nina's nostrils flared. 'No, Henry, it's definitely "aitch". Can you say that? "Aitch".'

'Mummy,' said Henry. 'At school Bevelly told me it's "haitch" for Henry.'

Nina made an appointment with the centre's manager, but once she was sitting down on the opposite side of the woman's desk, she realised there was nothing for her to say. Beverly was not a bad woman. Nina had never seen her be anything but sensible, calm and kind; and, now that Nina was here, it was clear to her that transmission of the letter sound 'haitch' to a two-and-a-half-year-old was not actually a matter of child abuse. And anyway, it wasn't the 'haitch'; it was Nina's sense that something within Henry was being damaged, even destroyed. It was Nina's desire to have someone, anyone, to blame. This was guilt. But Nina knew that the centre manager, with her practised gaze of professional concern, kept in the melamine drawers of her desk no magic cure for that.

☙

Back when Nina and Lucas borrowed the money for the extension on the house, Nina bought a fridge magnet with a 1950s cartoon couple in a clinch; the woman opening her perfectly lipsticked mouth to say, 'Darling, let's get deeply into debt'. It was still there on the fridge, holding up utility bills and head-lice notices, during the autumn Gracie turned one—and it was still there a few months later in the winter when Henry turned three, and still there a few weeks after that when Nina and Lucas silently colluded to allow their ninth wedding anniversary to slip by without ceremony or even remark. Although it had been a long time since Nina had found the fridge magnet amusing, she'd not got rid of it. It would have been so easy to slide it off the fridge, bend it until it snapped, toss it in the bin.

'I feel like debt is the only thing keeping us together,' Nina confided in Genevieve. 'If we separated . . . oh, God.'

When Nina thought of the debt, it was as an enormous concrete block that was being slid—long and thin, like a bank's safety deposit box—into its own purpose-built metal sleeve. It seemed to go on forever, and it left no space around its edges. Mortgage statements came in the mail and when Nina looked at the bottom line she realised that if the debt was a concrete monolith, they were working away at it with a squirt of Jif and a toothbrush. More than once Nina looked up the bankruptcy rules, taking all the secretive care that she would if she were trawling illicitly on RSVP.

'Separated?' Genevieve asked. 'You mean, you've thought about it?'

Of course she had thought about it. They spoke to each other, Lucas and she. Normal enough words came out of their mouths, but all Nina ever heard anymore was subtext. Lucas would ask, 'Is there any more milk?', but she heard, 'None of this would be so bad if we only had one child', and even as she said the words, 'You were supposed to get milk on the way home, remember?', she was filled with her own silent translation: 'Yeah, but who's the loser who fucked up the business, hmm?'

'Thought about it seriously?' Genevieve asked. 'Or are we in the ideation phase here?'

'Fairly seriously.'

'You know the rules,' Genevieve said. 'No separating until the youngest child is two years old. Those are the hardest years. Survive those and you'll be fine.'

Nina wondered where Genevieve got her information from and why she, Nina, had been denied access to this reliable and authoritative source, or its equivalent.

'Are you spending any time together, just the two of you?' Genevieve asked, but Nina's answer was just another of those bitter half-smiles that she was starting to worry would become her signature facial expression, the one that would craft the set of her midlife face and the wrinkles of her old age.

A few weeks later, Nina and Lucas's doorbell rang just after eight o'clock on a Saturday night. Nina opened the door to Genevieve who had with her an overnight bag, a rented movie and her dinner on a foil-covered plate.

'Go and get a frock on,' Genevieve said to Nina.

Genevieve found the remote control and flicked Lucas's footy match to mute.

'Take your wife out, man, and show her a good time. You've got until eight o'clock in the morning.'

Nina knew that Lucas liked Genevieve, even if he did mock her accent and bicker with her about politics. Genevieve sat at the other end of the couch from him, unzipped her long black boots and put her feet up. When he didn't move, she prodded him with a stockinged toe.

'And I'll have a glass of wine before you go. White, if you've got it. And not horse piss, either. Open something decent, alright?'

'*Ja, baas*,' said Lucas.

Ten minutes later, they were in the street; Nina standing there with her clutch purse and wrap feeling light-headed with freedom but also vaguely locked out of her own home. Lucas opened the passenger door of the big black Val and Nina stepped in, not quite remembering the way she was supposed to look at him over the door frame, or if there was anything in particular that she ought to say. She flicked on the interior light and in her compact mirror checked that her hurried swipe of lipstick wasn't on her teeth, that she hadn't blinked her mascara all over her eyelids or her cheeks. The mirror gave her back only pieces of herself: a dark eye forked at its edges with crow feet, a pair of lips and the surrounding skin that was starting to pleat. She wished she'd had time—or insisted on the time—to have a shower. Her hair wasn't so clean. She'd not shaved her legs for weeks and the stubble was pricking through her pantyhose. Even so, there was something familiar and sweet about the sensation of sitting in a full skirt on the ribbed leather of the bench seat, as well as in the old-car scent mix of rubber and oil combining with Lucas's additions of Minties and dope.

In the beginning, Lucas had come to her with the Val, and the Val had come to her with Lucas. It was black on the body, but white on the roof, and the horizontal silver bands of the front grille echoed the lines of the venetian blinds that were fitted to the rear and side back windows and that could close you in, close you out. It was in the back of the Val that Nina had trounced Janey Cooper once and for all. She and Lucas had both been too drunk and stoned to remember much about the night they first made love but, in the morning, they woke under Lucas's tawdry leopard-print blanket and once he threw that blanket off, it became apparent to him that Nina's body hair was not dark like the hair on her head. It was several shades lighter, thick and curling, a lush triangle lit by dusty stripes of venetian sunshine: red, gold, red, gold.

She had giggled at the astonished look on his face.

'That's *spectacular*,' he had said, then.

'Where do you want to go?' he asked now.

She knew, but it was no place you could get to twice. So they went to a movie, an art-house thing with lots of in-jokes about films Nina only barely remembered, throughout which neither Nina nor Lucas reached out to take the other's hand. They ate, late, at a restaurant about which everyone who still had a social life had been talking, and the food was very nice. At midnight they got back into the car.

'Well?' said Lucas.

'I don't know the name of a single nightclub anymore. I haven't a clue where's good.'

'You want to go to a nightclub?'

'Let's just go home,' Nina said.

'Think the *baas* will let us in?'

Nina shrugged. Lucas started up the Val and drove home. Their house was on the downhill side of the street and lately Nina had begun to suspect that it was inching further down the slope, sinking away towards the rivulet with all the weight of the world that occupied its four walls. Now she looked down at the cottage, the simple symmetry of its pitched roof, two square windows, rectangular front door. It sat there steadily behind its low, tidy picket fence and the idea of home settled upon Nina as if she had slipped on one of those leaden garments from an x-ray room; the heaviness felt almost right, as if her freedom from it had been nothing more than a delusion whose inevitable ending had come. It was Lucas whose senses rebelled. He turned the key in the ignition, lurched the big Val into a three-point turn.

Up and out he drove, through the steep outer suburbs to the bushy fringe of the city to a quiet place where you could see the big dark slash of the river between the light-jewelled hills. It wasn't exactly a lovers' lookout, or even a car park, just one of the many places where the city's roads ended at a padlocked boom gate, beyond which they became gravel tracks for walkers and cyclists. Nina didn't know what they were doing here and although she could tell that Lucas didn't either, she wasn't feeling generous enough to help him work it out.

He sat there for a while and then reached into his inside jacket pocket for the gloved-stitched leather tobacco pouch in which he always had at least a pinch of mull. He sifted out two papers, licked them together, laid out a bed of Champion Ruby and topped it with green. Nina watched his hands as he rolled: they were pale and freckled, the fingernails of his right hand long for plucking strings, those of his left bitten down to the quick, the matching stains between the index and middle fingers of both hands proving him an ambidextrous smoker. He lit up, passed to her. She inhaled, felt green smoke coil into her blood.

It was an old script, this one, and years since they had played it out, but at least they both knew it by heart. Turn by turn they smoked the joint down, Nina refusing at last, Lucas taking the burning roach between his fingers to inhale the dregs, scrunching his eyes and nose against the heat of the paper and tobacco on his lips. Then this hand went there, that tongue there; there was the same old slip and slide on the bench seat of the Val, the stretched sound of The Church on cassette tape in the stereo. Nina might have stopped there, but always it had been Lucas who decided when it was time to open the driver's side door, come around to the passenger side and invite her out with a courtly half-bow, the other half of which he saved for the gesture with which he ushered her into the back.

In the starlight Nina recognised that awful old leopard print blanket but she lay down on it anyway, reached up to close the venetians on her side. She let Lucas unbutton her dress, clumsily remove her tights; the dope and the kissing in the front seat did for foreplay. At first, they lay tight together chest to chest, but after a while he withdrew and nudged the outside of her thigh, suggesting she roll over onto her front. It was the way she had always liked it best, once. But now that she was the way she was—half heart-broken and dope-fogged—doing it this way made her into a fox bitch, orange and nasty. She felt rufous and ruined, her loose tits and belly like the sagging, teat-lined undercarriage of an overbred sheepdog. There was something degrading about it, but she came quickly anyway and he did too, although he was careful to pull out first. Instead of feeling any kind of afterglow she just cried.

'Do you still love me?' she asked, after a time.

'Of course I love you,' he said. 'Silly girl.'

Nina separated two dusty slats of the venetians and peeked out at a stripe of distant sky that might have been cloudy or just blurred by humans and all their vapours and foulness. She tried to imagine what it would be like to be with someone other than Lucas and it caused a painful twist inside of her. She knew she would always feel the nothingness where one of his qualities had been, or the something where there ought to have been a space. Yet it seemed to her that it was her ruination that bound her to him most tightly: the sagging and the stretching, the bitterness and the snappishness and the readiness to truly bite. He made those, those made her his. She rolled over, back into his arms.

'What's the worst of it, of how things are?' he asked her, and he sounded—or did she just want him to sound?—like someone wise, like someone who had the power to decide whether or not she deserved for the worst of it to be taken away.

'It's Henry,' she whispered into the scoop above Lucas's clavicle. 'I'm losing him. I'm losing him a little bit more every day. I know that this is how things are. I know this is what we have to do, but I wish, I just wish that I could go to work knowing that he was happy.'

At six o'clock each night, the doors of The Cottage were closed and its lights switched off. Nina had no idea what the staff did if parents didn't turn up in time to collect their children. She supposed that must happen sometimes. Unexpected things occurred in workplaces. There were accidents. There were parents who were no longer together and barely on civil terms; surely there must have been mix-ups when one or the other of them forgot whose turn it was. Even in this small city there was occasionally enough traffic—this night was a perfect example—to cause a delay.

But what happened to the children? Did the staff draw straws to see who would stay behind at the centre and wait until a parent, speeding and panicked and sorry, at last came hurtling in to the car park? But how long would the staff wait? And what would happen after that amount of time—however long it was—had elapsed? What if the parents couldn't be reached, found? Would Beverly eventually strap Henry and Gracie into her own car and drive them to the outer suburbs, take them into her home and sit them down on her couch and make them mugs of lukewarm Milo? Or would she at last put in a call to Children's Services, or the police?

Nina wondered and worried about all of this as she watched the bright green numbers on her dashboard clock spell out 6.10, 6.11, 6.12. It was spring by now and the days were lengthening; the evening sky, not yet fully dark, was pulsing with the flashing lights of emergency vehicles somewhere up ahead. Although Nina had remembered to plug her mobile telephone into its charger the previous night, she had somehow neglected to turn on the power point and by mid-afternoon the phone's battery was spent. She couldn't call The Cottage, she couldn't call Lucas; there were cars on three sides of her and a solid concrete crash barrier on the fourth. She thought of Henry and Gracie and wondered if they were sitting by the front door of the centre with their packed bags, waiting.

Slowly, slowly, infuriatingly slowly, the cars on the highway merged into a single lane and filed past the remains of the accident. Nina saw a bald man sitting on the rear step of the light-filled ambulance, his hands on either side of the bloodied gash to his scalp. Other people stood beside and between the two crumpled cars, talking on their mobiles or waiting with an air of suspended panic, their evenings having veered violently away from all expectations and plans.

It was 6.42 when Nina reached the centre. The car park was empty and the place looked blank and unfamiliar. No light came from the reception area, nor from any of the rooms whose windows faced the street, and yet the low, brick building somehow gave off the sense of a light still burning within. Nina hurried up through the avenue of toadstools to the glass doors. When they opened easily, she felt herself let out the breath that she had been half-holding for the past hour.

The light was coming from the end of the corridor, from one of the pre-kinder rooms that would next year be Henry's. Nina hurried past the pegged-up finger paintings and leaf rubbings and mosaics made from pasta bows, lengthening her stride as if she might outpace the thoughts that trailed her in a hectoring cloud. Henry would be four next year, the thoughts reminded her. It would be his last year before school. His early childhood was all but gone and it was she who had given it away. She would regret her choices, the thoughts said. She might have answered back that she already did, if it were not for her lingering suspicion that her regrets, like Henry himself, would never again be as small as they were today.

Nina rushed into the room through its wedged-open door, past the fridge that held the lunchboxes, past the low banks of open-faced lockers all marked with children's names, past the lost property trug brimming with hats and orphaned Tupperware lids, jumpers and odd socks. Beverly—it was Beverly who had waited—stood over by the sink in her navy pants and navy polo shirt, holding Gracie in place on her slightly out-thrust hip with one of her pale, doughy arms. Henry was sat on the sink-side bench, a plate strewn with crumbs and empty fairy-cake cases on his lap. He was the first to see Nina, the only one to look at her with reproach. Gracie smiled at her mother, unperturbed, and returned to her game of trapping in her hands the glossy beads on Beverly's spectacle chain, then pulling them into her little wet mouth.

'Henry. Sweetheart, I'm so sorry, the traffic . . . there was an accident . . .'

Nina reached out for Gracie, knowing that it was she herself, and not the little girl, who wanted and needed comforting. Beverly gave the child over, cleaned the glass of her smeared spectacles with the hem of her shirt.

'I'm so sorry,' Nina said to Beverly. 'I couldn't call . . . and it was gridlock . . .'

'These things happen,' Beverly said, with a smile and a shrug. 'And you'll get a bill.'

'I would have called but my phone . . . the battery was dead . . .'

Beverly was almost stubbornly calm and it made Nina feel foolish for the state she was in. Beverly turned to Henry as if demonstrating to Nina that he was, ought to be, their first and only concern.

'We were alright, weren't we, Henry?' Beverly said, her elbows on the bench beside his skinny little legs. 'We had fairy cakes, didn't we? And we said, didn't we, that Mummy would be alright? Didn't we say that Mummy would be along just as soon as she could?'

'No,' said Henry, to Beverly, clearly surprised she had forgotten. He looked to his mother, his face serious. 'I told her you had forgot us.'

What use were any of the platitudes? *Mummy would never leave you, Mummy would never forget you, Mummy will always be there.*

'Told,' whispered Nina. 'You told her.'

'All finished, mate?' Beverly asked, reaching out for his plate. 'Come on then, down you pop.'

'Thank you,' Nina said to Beverly, as she took Henry's hand. 'Thank you.'

'Don't mention it. Bye, Henry. Bye, Gracie possum.'

They reached the door leading out into the corridor before Henry broke his hand away from Nina's, ran back to the sink to throw his arms around Beverly's legs. He smiled up at her. 'Goodbye, Bevelly.'

Beverly leaned down to his height. 'See you tomorrow, Henry,' she said, touching a hand to his cheek.

'Promise?'

'You bet.'

Next morning before school when Nina frisked Henry on the front doorstep, she found not a single item stashed in any one of his many pockets.

𝕯

Quite some time has passed since then. Autumn has been— bringing with it Gracie's second birthday—and gone. It is early winter and soon Henry will turn four. The shortening days mean that it is already dark when Nina finishes work, cold and dark by the time she reaches The Cottage each evening. This night she sits outside the centre with her gloved hands on the steering wheel, listening to the stock market report she doesn't care about. For a while it is warm in the car. But not long after the engine has stopped, the warmth begins to leak out through the car's metal flanks, or the cold begins to seep in. Nina can't tell which. Perhaps both.

'Right,' she tells herself, breathes in.

There is already frost on the tiny hills and valleys of the gravelly path and as she steps onto it Nina can see herself in the dark of the double-glazed doors ahead. Surely it's a trick of the glass, and the distance, that she looks so thickset in her black coat and high-heeled boots. Could her end-of-the-day hair really be so tangled and skewed? At the sound of her step, a plaster bunny startles in the glow of a solar light; a hedgehog cowers beneath his toadstool.

'Look on the bright side, Nina. At least the mornings are easier,' Genevieve had said when Nina told her how things were now. Nina hadn't wanted to tell her. Genevieve's response had been deliberately droll, but the humour misfired.

'Come on, lovey,' Genevieve had said, when she had noticed the tears pooling in Nina's eyes. 'You've got to laugh or you'd spend your whole life crying.'

Nina knows that it is usually best to delay gratification and do the hardest job first, but when it comes to her evenings at The Cottage, she never does. Always, these days, she goes first to Gracie's room, and holds on for longer than she might otherwise when her daughter comes to her with her sticky little hands outstretched. Together they collect up drink bottle and lunchbox, spare clothes and the day's works of art, and zip them all into Gracie's ladybug backpack, which Gracie herself can carry on her back as she follows obediently behind Nina down the corridor to Henry's room. They do not hurry.

Soon enough Nina will get home with the kids, and a little after that Lucas will arrive, and husband and wife will resume the effort of not speaking to each other. Over the past months they had managed to get just a little way ahead, to chip from the debt a few small but honourable chunks. It was down to Nina, really, and Lucas would have admitted that. It was Nina who had sat up late at night writing blog posts for a pittance, and Nina who'd squeezed the grocery bill with her insistence on the no-name butter and cheese and the cheap nappies with the useless tabs that always wanted reinforcing with sticky tape. All that effort to be chimed away, all of it, in ten dollar bids the night Lucas was late home from work, and didn't answer his phone, and still wasn't back when Nina woke at 2.00 am with her heart trying to bash its way out of its cage. She'd put the kids in the car and covered them with bunny rugs, driven the usual haunts, until at last she'd found the big black Valiant in the car park of the Casino. Gracie had slept through the whole thing but Henry had sat in the back with his eyes wide open.

'Where you taking us?' he had asked. He had looked too scared even to blink.

But none of that is as bad as what is about to happen, and what happens every night. This is worse than the gambling, and the debt, and the no speaking—although in truth they are all wrapped up inside of it.

It begins the moment that Henry sees her.

'Go away. Go away, Mummy.'

Sometimes he runs away into the playground and hides, or pushes his back against the unlockable, downsized door of a toilet cubicle. Most usually, and this is what happens tonight, he clings to Beverly, wedging his fingers between her belt and her pants, wrapping his legs around her knee. Slowly, patiently, Beverly unhooks his fingers, prises away his limbs.

'Henry, Henry,' she says. 'It's time to go home with Mummy now.'

Beverly lifts him and holds him firmly to her. Although his face is red with crying and twisted with fury, her voice stays low and soft.

'We'll see each other again tomorrow, Henry. I promise.'

'I . . . I . . . I . . . want *you*. I don't want . . . h-h-h-her.'

'Cross my heart,' is all she says, but the invisible mark she makes with her finger is on Henry's chest.

Beverly puts Henry back on his feet but Nina knows by now that it's better she doesn't try to lift him herself. In the air he will kick. All the way back down the corridor, he will strike out with his feet at Nina, the walls, Gracie. So Nina has learned to hold him very firmly by the wrist and drag him, skidding, on his feet or on his knees. He is skinny, not at all strong, and nobody but she has to mend the jeans. She leaves her gloves on in case he bites.

'Come on, Henry,' Nina says, and she can taste the bitter stain on her words.

Gracie knows how to hold the door wide open so Nina can get Henry through.

'I don't want you, Mummy. I want Bevelly. Bevelly. Bevelly. I don't want you, Mummy. You're hurting me. Ow, ow, ow. You're hurting my arm,' he yells.

Nina has devised a way of closing herself down. She has built within her skull a system of airlocks to keep out the very worst of the humiliation and rage she feels as she drags her son along the corridor, past all the other parents: the ones who stare and the ones who look the other way.

'Bevelly. Bevelly. Bevelly. I want Bevelly, not you. I hate you. That hurts. It hurts. I hate you.'

At the car she has no choice but to lift him, but she has learned ways of wedging herself against the body of the car as she opens the door, and ways of keeping his legs pinned together where they can do less damage. She doesn't know what will happen when he learns how to extricate himself from the five-point harness that restrains him tightly enough that he can't kick the back of her seat or reach over to pull Gracie's hair.

During the drive home, Nina's hears the hiss of the airlocks opening, feels her soul sigh back into the uncomfortable cage of her bones. But she is determined to remain calm. Despite the thumping of Henry's fist on the side window, despite his frustrated cries, she will remain calm. She remains calm, she remains calm. She turns the radio back on even though she has spent all day with the same news of drownings from unseaworthy vessels, of job losses and their political fallout. She remains calm, but then misses the green arrow of a traffic light by one car's length and now she must wait. It's the sudden loss of momentum, the requirement that she sit, and sit, and sit, the sound of Henry's sobs seeping through the news of death and uncertainty and fear—that's what does it. She throws the gear lever into park, reefs on the handbrake. The heels of her boots scrape on the bitumen as she steps out of the car. She opens the back door and, to her shame, she strips off her glove before she slaps him. There is nothing muffled about the sound of her palm across the socket of his left eye, the upper margin of his cheek. She has hit him hard enough to feel the sting on the undersides of her fingers.

'Now shut up,' she screams at him. Her eyes and nose begin to stream with cold, misery. 'Shut. Up.'

Nina knows, of course, the senselessness of demanding that someone love you, just as she knows it is psychopathic to hurt someone because they will not. And now the arrow is green and queued up behind her car is a long line of other cars, their right-hand sides blinking in unsynchronised orange. There is a medley of car horns, but Nina—her red hand pressed against her son's raw cheek as if it might somehow suck the smack back out of his skin—cannot leave him now.

'I'm sorry, Henry. Mummy didn't mean to. I'm sorry. I'm sorry. Oh, Henry.'

But all he says, through his sobs, is 'Bevelly'.

Nina rocks back onto her heels, leans her head against the armrest of the opened door. The arrow is red again. Transmitting through the ether, conducting through the metal bodies of the cars is a current of banked-up anger from the drivers behind her. In her weepy eyes are the stripes and blurs of light that remain on the darkness as cars speed on, turn corners, convey their passengers homeward, while she remains lost. To be lost, to have lost; she has learned that the effect is much the same.

At home, Nina turns the key in the lock and the house breathes out breakfast-time air gone stale and cold over the length of the day. The first thing Nina does is to switch on the too-bright fluorescent in the hallway and twist Henry's small face up into the light. She doesn't think he will have a black eye. She hopes the finger-shaped marks across his temple and cheekbone will have faded by the morning, although she knows his memory will not have done.

'I'm so sorry, Henry. But you make me so . . .' She stops. There is no excuse. And he is not listening.

Nina turns on the television and Henry drifts towards the couch opposite. He is in his coat still, his dilated pupils catching the bright colours of the cartoon network even before she has found the button to give him some volume. He will not stir now. Not for half an hour at least, until he hears the Valiant sputtering down to stillness in the street. Then he will run for the door, calling 'Daddy!'. These days it's Lucas who helps Henry to brush his teeth and to find his pyjamas and Lucas who reads the bedtime story and tucks the covers down tight. After lights out, Nina hovers in the hallway, but only on her bravest days, and certainly not on this day, will she venture in to kiss her son goodnight.

She still has Gracie, though—little Gracie who is following after her mother into the kitchen. Lately, Nina has been teaching her to cook. Now Gracie reaches down her own small apron with ric-rac around the pockets. She slides on the tiny pair of padded oven gloves from the hook which also holds Nina's. Two-year-old Gracie has learned which knobs will switch the oven on, and how to watch for the light that will tell her it's hot enough, and how to open the door and reach in without hurting herself. Nina and Gracie haven't bothered much with cupcakes or gingerbread cookies or puddings. It's flesh Nina wants to smell roasting.

On weekends, Nina and Gracie cook whole birds: chicken, spatchcock, quail, even a duck if there's one on special, but tonight it's only chicken pie to be warmed through.

'I do it,' Gracie says, and Nina smiles.

Carefully, Gracie hinges open the oven door. With two hands and a concentrating tongue between her teeth, she slides the pie in its foil bed into the still-cold heart of the oven, shuts it in. When it is done, Nina puts up her hand, the same one she used to hit Henry—and the skin of it still tingles—for a high five.

'Can we do one tonight, Mummy?' Gracie asks, looking up at the windowsill. 'Can we? Can we please?'

'Why not?' Nina says, lifting her up to sit on the bench. 'You go ahead and choose.'

On the sill, beside the dishwashing liquid and a potted cactus, is a parade of wishbones. They have been picked clean of every last little thread of meat and left to dry in the sun. Gracie has arranged them from largest to smallest, placing them on their curving backs so that she can make them rock as she names each one.

'This is the daddy, this is the mummy, this is the big brother, and this is me,' Gracie says, setting the quail's bone in motion.

'Which one tonight, darling?'

'That one,' she giggles, then leans over the lip of the kitchen servery to look down at Henry where he sits on the couch, knees drawn up to his chin.

But Nina, heartsick with the aftermath of the day's end, says, 'Maybe a different one?'

'This one?' Gracie says, pointing to the biggest of the chicken bones.

That's my girl, thinks Nina.

Together she and Gracie link their little fingers through the wishbone's delicate arch.

'Are you ready?' Nina asks.

Gracie nods, puts out her concentrating tongue.

'One, two . . . three!'

But Nina will pull only softly, if at all. Although she will enjoy the splintering crack, she wants the bigger side to fall to Gracie. It's been quite some time now since Nina has trusted herself with anything so precious as a wish.

sleep

You reach womanhood and although there may not be a spindle,
there will still be blood, a curse, and some little prick.

IN THE STATELY home next door lived old Mrs Bunting and her unmarried daughter, Rita. The ground floor and the first floor were Mrs Bunting's exclusive domain, while the top floor had been converted into a flat for Rita. That was about forty years ago when Mrs Bunting realised Rita would never be normal.

Rita dressed like a bag lady, which is what she would almost certainly have become if her mother hadn't given her an allowance and a place to live on the top floor of a riverside mansion. Rita had a separate entrance at the top of a staircase at the back of the house, and there was a view of it from the bay window in Liv's room.

Liv had never heard anyone label Rita Bunting or her particular problem, the symptoms of which included a slack jaw, bad teeth, layered rolls of fat around her middle and a sly, obstreperous manner. Although conversation was possible, Rita's half of it came back to you as if refracted through a prism, one that seemed to tilt, or spin. The same thing that delighted her today would tomorrow make her scowl darkly and start cussing like a sailor. Even in the dialogue Rita held with herself, she covered the full spectrum. Sometimes Liv would hear her crooning in a high, wheedling tone; other times she would berate herself in a fluctuating growl that made Liv think of someone twiddling a volume switch.

Lauren didn't get a view of Rita's door. Her bedroom was across the hall from Liv's and faced the wrong way. It had no bay window either. Being the younger sister, Lauren thought, was a bit like turning up in the afternoon to a garage sale once all the good stuff was gone. A year and a half older than Lauren, Liv had got the pick of the family's heirloom books and toys and crockery, and exercised her first-born right to name the grandparents. By the time Lauren started music lessons, Liv had already been playing the violin for a year and a half. Lauren quickly learned that 'viola' was just another way of saying 'second fiddle'.

Even Rita paid more attention to Liv than she did to Lauren. Sometimes Rita accosted the girls at their front gate, or in the driveway, or right down at the bottom of the garden where the fence between the properties petered out into lawn. She addressed her strange directives to both girls, but it was Liv she would beckon in most closely. Sometimes she would even grab hold of Liv's arm as she spoke.

'You must not flush toilets at night,' she had warned them, once. 'The sound of the pipes attracts . . . men.'

Occasionally she was confrontational. One time she accused Liv and Lauren of having orgies in their bedrooms. 'I've *heard* you,' she said.

There was a story that Rita wasn't always this way. People who were old enough to remember, including Liv and Lauren's grandmother, said Rita had once been quite ordinary, even somewhat pretty, right up until the night of her twenty-first birthday party. This party had been described to Liv and Lauren as a 'society event'. Liv pictured it with gilt-edged invitation cards, a tower of coupe champagne glasses, women in fox fur stoles and waiters with white gloves. When it was said that Rita sat down at the end of that night in her ballgown and said, 'That's it, my life is over now', Liv liked to imagine that this took place on the big formal staircase with curving banisters of dark polished wood that she had seen leading up into a gallery from Mrs Bunting's entrance hall, but that Liv had never herself ascended. Liv envisioned Rita seated about halfway up those stairs, sitting in her foaming skirts of pale pink tulle, a tiara in her hair.

Lauren and Liv's house had no grand central staircase. Their place was just as big as the Buntings', but newer, more airy, less Miss Havishamish. Theirs had been built for Liv and Lauren's grandfather, the second in the political Wishart dynasty, and when he died he had handed the house on to his son—Liv and Lauren's father—who also ended up taking over the family seat in parliament. It so happened that about the time Liv's eighteenth birthday was approaching, their father caught the sniff of an election on the breeze. He suggested a party. Their mother began making lists.

In the small city in which they grew up, Liv—more than Lauren—was known to people. This was in part because she was talented and had played her violin in public since she was very young, and in part because the city was small and she conspicuous. Liv was slender (Lauren slightly less so) and gave the impression of being tall, although she was not especially, and she had the kind of posture that spoke quite accurately of family money. Liv never intended to appear imperious, but with her ballerina neck and the way she pulled her long hair back over her neatly moulded skull, she did.

Lauren and Liv were quite obviously sisters, but when Lauren looked in the mirror she saw the results of a follow-up experiment that had failed to replicate the spectacular results of the first. Still, she would not have wanted to be Liv. She knew, even at the age of sixteen and a half, there was something about her own thicker bones and coarser features that kept her just this side of a particular kind of danger. She also knew that if Liv had so far got more than her fair share, well, that was just Liv. She was the last person in the world with whom you would want to be trapped within a disabled submarine: somehow she would even manage to breathe two-thirds of the air.

Invitations to the party went out to everyone the Wisharts knew.

'That's it, my life is over now,' Liv started to say, each time she descended the stair between the top floor and the first floor of their home. She tried out various attitudes—woeful, dramatic, bitter, pathetic—but Lauren didn't like it any which way.

'Don't,' Lauren said. 'Just, please, don't.'

In Liv's room, everything hard was painted white and everything soft was ruffled around the edges. The curtains were blue gingham, there was a pile of artfully mismatched blue and white cushions on the window seat, and a wicker chair full of antique rag dolls that had only ever been for show. Liv liked to get away from all this. She wasn't sure how deeply her parents believed her when she said was staying over with Claudia, or Annabel, or Freya: girls whose parents were known to her own, but not too well.

Liv could sleep anywhere: on beer-sloshed after-party couches and beanbags, on car seats, in the backs of camper-vans, and in the warm nicotine grime of any number of beds that were available to her should she be prepared to share. Lately, since she had got in with a crowd of musicians who hung out around the waterfront and busked their filthy sea-shanties for hats-full of coin, her bed of choice was a bunk on a small boat. When it was in port, she would lie with her lover in the coffin space beneath the vessel's prow and hold him tight to her chest, fingering silent tunes on the nodules of his vertebrae, just as his own fingers flurried over the black buttons of his piano accordion. She slept well there, even though there was nothing but a thin shell of paint and planking to separate her from the harbour and the slapping of its waves.

But she woke on the morning of her eighteenth birthday party in her own bed in the blue room with the view over the garden, the river, and Rita Bunting's front door. Through bleary eyes and dewy glass, she could see her mother, queenly in her quilted dressing gown, plucking bruised petals from the late blooming camellias as she criss-crossed the lawn. June Wishart was—to Liv—a kind of first position, the default against which mothers of all other sorts were defined. If Liv sometimes looked hungrily at the mothers with long, messy curls and jeans—the ones who kissed and hugged their grown daughters and made easy, stupid jokes with them, borrowed their earrings and shoes—it was only within an understanding of how far they deviated from June Wishart with her ash blonde hair that rolled under, quite naturally, at her jaw, who always wore skirts and never went out without pantyhose, whose public manner towards her daughters was just one or two notches more intimate than the cheerful, well-brought-up formality with which she treated everyone else.

Liv watched June as she walked down past the bungalow at the bottom of the garden, all the way to the water's edge, to the place where the grassy bank rolled neatly into the river like a swimmer at the end of a lap. And even from where she sat at the second-storey window, Liv could feel her mother's absolute riverfront satisfaction.

☞

On the back of Liv's door had appeared, while she slept, her dress for the party. Handmade for the occasion by her mother, it was beautifully pressed and hanging on a padded coathanger. The matching shoes waited obediently, heels together, against the battered black of her violin case. She knew that it would be the same in Lauren's room, although the fabric of the button-through frock would be a different dainty floral print and the shoes—in a different but equally insipid pastel shade—would be set out beside Lauren's viola case.

June had budgeted for twelve of Liv's own friends at the party, but Liv had chosen not to invite a single one. She wouldn't have known how to manage her own friends while at the same time being buttoned into a dress like that and handing around hors d'oeuvres. So long as her friends were not there, she was fairly sure she would be able to pack one of her selves down flat, slide it into a narrow space, unseen.

When the guests began to arrive, Liv watched Lauren slip effortlessly into character. Her little sister did not require ironic distance to carry trays, or listen attentively to the bland and diplomatic answers that were produced by her bland and diplomatic questions. Lauren was good. And on this day, Liv knew she ought to be good, too.

From one of the caterers she received a platter of pickled baby octopus and was revolted and amused by the piles of tiny rubbery pink bodies, which she thought would make rather good novelty nose-plugs. She congratulated herself on resisting the urge to shove one up each nostril before venturing out onto the lawns for her first tour of duty. Instead she just fixed her mouth into a slightly manic smile, and sashayed out into the gardens.

'And how is Josephine?' Liv asked. And, 'Have you been making the most of the lovely weather?' and, 'Will you ski, this winter?' When one of her father's colleagues peeked down her cleavage while his fat fingers hovered over the octopus plate, she was beset with an urge to drop the plate, tear open her perfectly pressed bodice, unhook the centre clasp of her bra to reveal her trim little breasts and say, 'Have a proper look, why don't you, George?' Instead, she just held her platter a little higher where it obscured George's view.

Toby Bourke was not a person of especial interest to Liv. If you had mentioned his name to her, she would have thought of the very little boy he had once been, and remembered how she and his older brother scared him during a game of hide and seek, locking themselves in the bungalow to play a game of doctors and nurses that left them both with smelly fingers and racing hearts. And yet here he was, wishing her a happy birthday and leaning over the baby octopus to kiss her on the cheek, having somehow morphed into a fifteen-year-old young man who knew how to *flirt*. She smelt his overdosed aftershave, felt his ever-so-slightly raspy cheek-skin against hers. She scanned the lean length of his torso through the fabric of his pale blue shirt (new, obviously, without the packaging creases ironed out of it), but reminded herself that, today, she was going to be good.

Liv had heard of a thing called Tourette syndrome and sometimes she wondered if she had it. Or at least a touch of it. She was always thinking of doing strange things. Strange, stupid, childish things, like reaching out and sticking her finger up somebody else's nose. Back in the kitchen to collect a fresh platter, she caught sight of her birthday cake and thought about scratching something obscene into its smooth blanket of royal icing. While she was standing with ladle in hand behind the punch bowl, lifting the dainty crystal cups off the hooks around its circumference, she imagined herself lowering her face right into the sweet liquid and blowing bubbles, coming up with a mouthful of punch and squirting it in a high pink plume over her head. When the adults started playing croquet (*croquet*, for fuck's sake, could her mother have dreamed of anything more affected?), Liv wanted to leap out onto the pitch, drop her daks and lay a colossal turd, rotating her hips in big round circles so that the shit would come out like soft-serve on a Mr Whippy cone.

It wasn't that Liv exactly wanted to do any of these things; it was more that she worried that she might. To be on the safe side, Liv took a break from serving duties and took herself off towards the bottom of the garden, where a wrought-iron bench had been positioned in a secluded spot behind a screen of young pines. On this bench sat her grandmother—her mother's mother—smoking. Liv sat down beside her and, without asking, helped herself to one of the Alpine cigarettes that Babs had transferred from their cardboard packet to a white Glomesh case. Babs gave her granddaughter the disapproving look that was an essential part of this transaction, then lit Liv's cigarette with the slender flame from a silver-cased lighter.

'Why thank you, Grandmamma.'

'All the better to kill you with.'

When Liv was born, Babs—whose actual name was Cath—had not wanted to be Nanna or Granny, so June had chosen 'Nanette' as a sensible approximation. But Liv had called her Babs. For at least a couple of years, June tried to stick to the original plan, asking 'Where's Nanette?', saying 'Go to your Nanette', writing 'With Nanette' in the photograph albums, and 'From Nanette' in the front covers of books given at Christmas-time. But to Liv, for no particular reason that anyone could discern, her grandmother was Babs, and never anything else but Babs, and these days she was Babs to virtually everyone.

Babs no longer lived in their small city but in a larger, warmer city to the north, where she had moved after her second husband died. Liv, far more often than Lauren, had been sent up north for holidays with Babs, and these were trips, full of sky and glass and sun, from which Liv always felt that she came back down, literally, to earth. Babs, who lived in an apartment on the thirteenth floor, seemed to conduct all of her socialising and shopping at a similar altitude, lowering herself to street level only in transit.

'I suppose there will be a musical interlude today?'

'Perfect, accomplished daughter number one, at your service,' Liv said, making a curling gesture in smoke on the air.

'And how are things, oh accomplished one, at le conservatoire?'

'Actually,' Liv said, on the drawback breath, then exhaled, 'I've decided not to go back next year.'

Liv was not certain this was true, but she thought she would try it on as a fact rather than the embryonic fancy it still was.

'Really?'

'Yes,' said Liv. 'I can hardly wait to break the news to June.'

It pleased Liv and Babs to agree that their particular personality was one that had skipped a generation and that June's quite different one might sometimes require analysis and discussion. And she was always 'June' when Liv was in this mood. Liv supposed her mother was easier to talk about if stripped of her office first.

'Speaking of whom,' Liv said, 'what did you say to her? She's been chewing the corner of her lip ever since you came downstairs this morning.'

'Well, she asked me,' Babs said. 'She said, "Do you like my

dress?" And I told her it looked like something that might be accessorised with a commode.'

'You terrible old bitch.'

'Hussy. Speaking to your aged grandmother like that.' Babs ground her spent cigarette between an elegant white wedge heel and a paving stone. 'So, if not music, what *are* you going to do?'

'I'm going to do whatever one does do, nowadays, in place of running away with a circus. What would that be, do you think?'

'Darling, I'm hardly up with the latest.'

'What about exotic dancing?'

'Quite exerting, I would have thought. Sweaty.'

From beyond the screen of pines came the sound of a woman squealing joyfully, a man's laughter. Perhaps he had tickled her, or spilled her drink.

'I see Charlotte the harlot is here,' Liv said.

'Yes, poor love. She really must stop drawing her eyebrows on with a compass. It makes her look so terribly surprised.'

'Why *does* June invite her?'

'I suppose she thinks your father wants her here. I suppose she thinks that's the kind of thing a Good Wife does. Perhaps she thinks it's better if it's right under her own nose.'

'Do you reckon Lottie and Daddo, you know, at things like this . . . do you think they rendezvous somewhere in the house for a quickie?'

'Olivia Wishart!'

'Well, do you?'

'I can't imagine where you learned to be so vile. I'm off to the powder room to avoid your contaminating influence.'

Getting to her feet, Babs smiled both tartly and proudly, while Liv swung her feet up on to the seat and began to hum.

✿

Liv and Lauren had agreed to play Mozart's *Duo for Violin and Viola in B flat major*. And, for a while, they did. On white Bentwood chairs, with the rose garden as a backdrop, within a treble-tiered semi-circle of seats that had been put out for the older guests, the sisters sat in their floral dresses, shook back their ponytails—Liv's very fair, Lauren's not quite so—lifted their instruments under haughtily held chins, and played. Not everyone chose to listen. Lauren could see little clusters of guests scattered the length of the garden, laughing and talking; she could see her father pressing the flesh at the drinks table.

It was mostly the older ladies, their mother's friends and the ones with season tickets for the orchestra, who gathered for the entertainment. Lauren worried about the way they swayed to the music. With their heads of sprayed hair, brittle and tacky as fairy floss, they might easily stick if they didn't all go the same way. Lauren smiled, and Liv smiled too, as if this thought had climbed up to her on one of the staircases of notes that the viola was building for the violin to dance on. In time, pitch-perfect, they played so well together, the Wishart girls. Everyone said so.

A few bars into the second movement, Lauren noticed Charlotte Simpson take one of the unoccupied chairs at the end of a row. Charlotte was something of a mystery to Lauren. She sometimes evened up the numbers if their mother was having a big sit-down dinner, and she always came to their parties. She wore clothes that floated a little way off her thin limbs and she made up her face the way a child might, with circles of pink on her cheeks and black mascara clotting her pale lashes. Charlotte always made Lauren think of thistledown, blowing around in the breeze and clinging to things. She was apt to be found attached to the sleeve of someone's jumper, or—if she'd had one too many glasses of white wine—in their lap.

When Lauren caught a change in the sound of the violin, it was neither in the tempo nor the volume. She looked over at her sister and thought instantly of the Cheshire cat. She could almost see the tail, long and striped, curling out from beneath Liv's backside, its tip twitching in anticipation. Liv did not return Lauren's questioning glance, but she wasn't looking at her sheet music either; she was watching Charlotte Simpson, pupils dilated, gaze focused in the way of a feline about to spring. The Mozart that was coming off her strings was still delicate and playful, but also edgy, faintly menacing. Lauren looked to June, but her mother had herself tightly in check, her face tucked in tight around all its edges, betraying nothing.

Liv got to her feet, still watching poor cornered Charlotte, and whatever it was that she was playing now, it was no part of the *Duo for Violin and Viola in B flat major.* Lauren let her viola's sound trail away. She laid her bow and her instrument on her lap, smiled reassuringly at the audience, and Liv—still playing her fiddle—shaped her body to a sailor's jig, knees and elbows pumping. To the roistering tune, electric with mischief, she skipped from side to side wildly enough to pop the bottom two buttons from her new dress and Babs, beneath the broad white brim of her hat, laughed. Toby Bourke was standing at the back of the seating banks and Lauren could see that Liv's music was pulsing through him; he might even have been tapping a toe in time. Then Liv, in the clear, true voice that for years had annually brought home a blue ribbon from each of the city's three separate eisteddfods, began to sing:

> *Charlotte the harlot lay dying, a pisspot supporting her head,*
> *Surrounded by horny old noblemen, she rolled on her left tit and said,*
> *'I've been fucked by dear George in his office, I've been fucked by that*
>   *balding QC,*
> *'Now I've come over here to this party, to fuck Mr Wishart MP . . .'*

At which point Clive Wishart stepped in, the skin of his face and neck taut with blood. He took hold of the neck of the violin—Liv's hand still upon it—and silenced her.

Lauren could not have said who alerted or summoned him. It was not Charlotte Simpson; she had left, almost running down the side of the house, out towards the street, speaking to nobody on the way. Women were gathered around June, comforting her, collecting up details; and Lauren, not knowing what else to do, lifted her viola and launched into the *Prelude* of Bach's *Suite No. 1*.

Ever after, Lauren would continue to love this prelude, as she loved it then. But she would never again hear or play its stirring, see-sawing phrases without thinking of her father marching her sister past those banks of chairs, up the veranda steps and into the house, of the birthday cake that never made it out of the kitchen, and of the tense, determined way Liv's party went on without her.

Still in her dress, on top of the covers, hair loosed from its ponytail, the door of her bedroom untouched since her father had closed it on her with something just short of a slam, Liv slept. She slept knowing that the party would come to an end, that several mauve-haired women who had drunk too much sherry would drive slowly and dangerously home in their pug-nosed hatchbacks, that a coterie of men would linger downstairs with her father and the single malt, and that sooner or later her mother would come up to her room to administer The Talk. Resistance was futile. June could have reiterated for the nation, and Liv knew from long experience that the only way to shorten The Talk was to agree. Yes, she would say, her behaviour was appalling. Yes, she would say, she understood that the Wishart family's reputation was money in the bank.

Sleep has layers but Liv could not seem to get past its shallows where she could still hear sounds from the world beyond and watch how artfully they threaded themselves into her half-conscious dreams. Although Liv could not have said precisely how much time had passed, when a knock came at her door she knew it was sooner than expected. She kept her eyes closed and sent her thoughts back out in search of the sleep that might, if she was lucky, put The Talk off until tomorrow. The door opened. She felt the weight of a body on the edge of her bed: not at the end, though, where her mother would sit, but closer, right up in the foetal curve of her body.

Somebody, with a finger that was hot and hesitant, guided a strand of her hair away from her cheek, making a clear space on which to land a light, raspy kiss.

'What *are* you doing?' Liv said.

But Toby Bourke held his nerve, even smiled. 'I found these,' he said. 'I thought you might want them back.'

In his hand were two buttons. She sat up, took them from him, and then—watchful of him, curious—set them down on her bedside table.

'That was pretty wild down there,' he said.

She considered, weighing her options. She had to admire his courage. Also, sex would help her get back to sleep. She wrapped her hand around the back of his skull and pulled his face towards hers. The suction of his kiss dragged her lips right into his mouth and made a noise a bit like straw at the bottom of a milkshake.

'Jesus, watch it.'

'Sorry.'

'Like this,' she said, clamping his head between her hands and pulling away from him every time he got too keen.

She couldn't tell which was more pleasurable, the feel of his hot sweaty hands, or his delighted disbelief when she allowed him to put them wherever he liked. She pushed him gently onto his back, reefed at his belt buckle.

'You do want . . . ?'

He nodded.

'You have done this before?'

'Sure.'

Liv freed the slender, bendy young stem of his cock from his pants. It reminded her, almost disgustingly, of a Vienna sausage, the skin a bit baggy and peeling at its tip. She stripped off her knickers and spread the flared skirt of her dress out over his chest and hips and thighs. Not quite, she thought, the use her mother had had in mind.

☙

When Liv woke again it was from a deeper kind of sleep that washed through the lobes of her brain like salt water: wave after clean, rinsing wave of it. The last of the day's light was sliding out of the sky and from her window seat she could see her mother crossing and recrossing the lawn with trays of leftovers, fingersful of sherry glasses, a garbage bag for the emptied bottles and serviettes. The Talk was overdue by now. Also, Liv had begun to feel a little sorry.

In bare feet she descended two flights of stairs, went out through the hall, across the veranda and down onto the lawn, her toes feeling the cool evening wetness of the thick-bladed grass. She walked in the direction of the river, near to her mother. She loitered, inviting eye contact and when it did not come, she dallied by a table, flicked away some spilled food, folded the soiled tablecloth neatly into sixteenths. But her mother did not speak to her, or even look at her, only continued steadily on her ant-track between lawn and house.

'Mum?'

June looked chilly even in her cardigan; the shadows under her eyes were like bruises, and for this Liv felt responsible. Liv had grown to the same height as her mother. She was too big now to lay her head against her mother's chest and feel safe and forgiven.

'There's nothing you can say, Liv,' June said, already walking back to the house. 'Nothing that wouldn't be total bullshit.'

Liv stood for a moment watching her mother walk away, then wandered all the way down to the river's edge, lifted the skirt of her dress and stepped into the water with both feet. It was cold and she thought of how she must look standing there: as if she had been sliced off at the ankles by the steely still water. She thought, too, of the river and how it only seemed to be standing still, while in fact it was pouring itself invisibly out to sea.

⅋

Curses take their own sweet time and for quite a while Liv remained unaware that she had fallen beneath one. That summer, she spent her days at the waterfront, on the foredeck of a permanently anchored ketch, playing music. She and her fiddle learned new songs, forgot the old prissiness, made merry with piano accordions, tin whistles and the spoons. For the holiday crowds, Liv in her torn-off denim shorts played hard and fast, powdered resin rising in a white cloud from her strings as she sawed serrated notes through the afternoons and on until the sun set.

'Isn't that Olivia Wishart?' people would sometimes say, but the crowds were made up mainly of tourists, and of local families briefly unhitched from the year's school-and-work routine, not people who knew her.

The boat never moved, tethered as it was in a concrete sea, but Liv vomited into the scuppers anyway. Her fellow buskers held back her hair, gave her water to sip and salt crackers to nibble, helped her back onto her feet, kept playing. Her accordion-playing lover sailed away in his wooden boat, after one night shaping his hands to Liv's bare and billowing belly. Even so, that she was pregnant was not something Liv was ready to admit. For a good many weeks after the idea occurred to her, she trusted that her suspicions were nothing more than irrational fears that would pass. For all the time that she half-heartedly worried in the back of her mind, she also kicked herself for not taking more care, and for being stupid enough to think—insofar as it was actually a thought and not just an ill-formed notion—that because Toby Bourke was as harmless as a kitten that his sperm was also.

$\mathcal{D}$

In was late summer and the waterfront crowds had thinned; Liv decided to make use of the airfare that her grandmother had given her for her birthday. Babs no longer came to collect Liv from the airport. Liv knew her way on trains and buses through the city and out into the harbour-side suburb full of shrubs and trees and vines that ambushed all the fences, sprouting new shoots of life in every direction, studded with flowers in shades of pink, purple and magenta that would seem unthinkably crass back at home. Even the parrots here chirruped with more confidence. Although it was hotter, it didn't matter: Liv felt the soft shelter of ozone, the smoothness of the damper air on her skin and in her lungs as she walked the last few blocks. In the uncultivated gardens by the wayside were disorganised vines hung with pods large enough to eat small children; at the entrance to Babs's apartment block was a colossal, spiny cactus that Babs had told her flowered only once in a hundred years.

On the smoky glass table on her balcony Babs had set out an orange poppyseed cake and two tumblers of iced water with slices of lemon and mint sprigs. Babs's glassy apartment contained not a single extraneous thing. Already she had

made a ruthless accounting of her needs and had thrown
almost everything away. On the white walls were only the
most beloved of her art works; her slimline shelves held only
a few framed pictures, no ornaments, a single photograph
album. She had started to read on a Kindle. All evidence of
the baking of the orange poppyseed cake had been cleared
away behind the spotless silvery surfaces of the kitchen, but
Liv caught sight of the top corner of the packet mix cake box
poking out of the bin.

'You slack tart.'

'Don't tell June on me, will you?'

'What's it worth to you?' Liv said, although she could
already tell that their patter was falling short of its usual
spiritedness. Babs seemed pensive; Liv wondered if she were
unwell, or had got some bad news.

They ate cake and shared harmless gossip, but when Liv
reached out for the white Glomesh case of cigarettes on the
veranda railing, Babs's thin hand in its glove of fine, wrinkled
skin landed on top of hers. 'I don't think that's a good idea,'
Babs said. 'Do you?'

What was that look on Babs's face? It was knowingness,
and sympathy, and perhaps just a touch of hurt. Liv thought
of something that passed between them when she was very
young. Although Babs too must have been much younger
then, she had already seemed ancient on the day that Liv,
wild with jealousy that Lauren was going out alone for lunch
with Babs, had driven her small white teeth into the fragile,

sunspotted skin of Babs's hand. The bite had drawn blood. But Babs had only taken her hand back, looked at Liv with pained understanding and said, 'I know, sweetheart, I know.'

Now, she said, 'Best be good, under the circumstances, hmm?'

And Liv felt fall into alignment a series of lenses that she had been keeping quarantine in separate quarters of her mind. An uncompromising beam of light now shone on the equally uncompromising fact that she was expecting a child. She looked at her body and realised how much she had been trusting in the stories of women who had got away with it for the whole nine months and surprised everyone, at the last moment, by whipping a baby out from under their loose-fitting dresses. Or else bundled their suffocated babies in a bloodied tangle of sheets and shoved them deep in the laundry hamper. But slender and light-framed as she was, she now saw that at five months gone she was well beyond the point at which any trick of pleating or draping could actually hide her shape.

'Are you terribly disappointed with me?'

'Darling girl.'

Babs shook the cigarettes from the Glomesh case into her hand, took them to the bin and crumbled them into uselessness. 'It's about time I gave up anyway,' Babs said. 'June always says so.'

'Oh God,' said Liv. 'June.'

'I could be the one to tell her,' Babs said. 'If you think that would be best. If she has some time to think before you get home, it might, perhaps, soften the blow.'

The bed in Babs's white spare room ought to have been an oasis of sleep. Getting into it that night, clean from the bath, Liv felt the layers of feathered softness beneath her, on top of her, in the pillow upon which she lay her head. She waited for sleep, searched for it. She tried diving down into it, but she was too buoyant. Perhaps it was this new swollen stomach of hers anchoring her to the surface like a glass ball full of air. After a few hours, she got out of bed.

Liv was as quiet as possible as she opened the bathroom door and closed it again behind her. The mirrored door of the bathroom cabinet opened with only the smallest of clicks. She was careful not to rattle the small white bottle of Temazepam that Babs kept there, but slipped her finger inside to capture two white pills, put her mouth to the tap before easing it on to the barest drizzle. And yet, somehow she had disturbed Babs, who was standing in sheeny white pyjamas in the hallway when Liv let herself back out of the bathroom.

'Can't sleep?' Babs said.

'Not really.'

Liv had not known she was close to tears, but now a small sob leapt up into her throat like a hiccup.

'Darling. Why don't you come in with me?'

Babs tucked Liv into her own bed, climbed in beside her. And after a while sleep did come to Liv, but it was not the kind she was looking for. There were no pale hands reaching up, helping her down into the deep. This sleep was a decompression chamber, restrictive and dreamless, and she woke from it still tired, as if some shut-off part of her had remained awake all along.

The Talk took place in the blue room. June pushed aside the rag dolls and perched on the wicker chair; Clive sat, arms folded, on the window seat. When Liv refused to name names, Liv could see that this infuriated Clive, who had obviously hoped to be able to share some of the disapprobation with another family. June, though, seemed content for the truth to remain where it was and Liv wondered what her mother feared more: that the baby's father was some unsavoury musician type who Liv had picked up at the waterfront, or that he would turn out to be someone like, or even precisely, George.

The lack of an identifiable father, however, altered few of the details that Clive and June had already worked out. Liv would move out of the house and into the bungalow and Clive—who could not afford to have a daughter of his sucking on the public teat—would give Liv an allowance that was precisely equal to the single parent benefit, minus a reasonable percentage for the rent that was already covered by the provision of the bungalow. Liv would be quite well set up, really, with a place to live and a modest income. When the baby was a year old, Clive would withdraw the allowance and

Liv could get a job and support herself, either in the bungalow (he wouldn't charge her the full market value, obviously) or somewhere else. Although the beginning of the academic year was upon them (Lauren had already returned for her final year at school), the Conservatorium was never mentioned.

'Well?' said June.

It wasn't a question, or even a dare, so much as it was a demand for Liv to argue, reject their benevolence, or in some other way crack the fragile seal of her mother's pre-prepared fury. But Liv only nodded mutely. She was apprehending something greater, even, than her mother's disappointment. She felt as if she had been walking backwards through a familiar world in which choices were between chocolate chip and peppermint, and consequences were two weeks without pocket money or a friend in a sulk; all the punishments she was familiar with were soon forgotten, or at the very least easily reversed by apologies and promises of reform. But now she had turned around and felt the cold wind of an entirely new landscape, lunar and forbidding, full of unimaginably large things, solid and irreversible.

❦

The bungalow had been built a little while after the big house, but the builders had made a good fist of matching up the dark red variegated bricks and of replicating the scrolled sandstone aprons beneath the windows. The scale of the buildings was so disparate, however, that the bungalow seemed related to the house in a cute and almost mocking way, as if the bungalow were the house's lap dog or novelty handbag.

Guests had stayed in the bungalow in recent years, but only if June was putting up a great many people all at once. If there were just one or two couples, they would stay in the guest rooms on the first floor of the house: these had en suites and furnishings that had been kept up to date. The bungalow had been redecorated by Clive's mother in a fit of modernity in the early 1980s and between that time and the time of Liv's pregnancy was an interval of precisely the wrong duration; none of the fittings or furnishings—not the ceramic doorhandles painted with rosebuds, nor the gilt-embellished picture rails, nor the damask drapes—had been given enough time to come back into any sort of vogue, tongue-in-cheek or otherwise. The couches, their bosomy cushions upholstered in dusky pink velvet, bulged in the bungalow's living room like two enormously fat naked women.

In the house, June had got rid of all the evidence of Clive's mother's tendency to skimp, but had never quite made it to the bungalow, where the carpet was still acrylic and the crystal-plastic taps in the kitchen and bathroom tended to drip. From deep in the soft furnishings came a cold and unlived-in smell that was not alleviated by opening windows that had been placed without regard for the movement of the sun. On the walls closest to the riverbank the paintwork above the skirting boards bloomed grey, blue and green.

Liv had not been clear that she was supposed to move in to the bungalow straight away, but on the day immediately following The Talk, she came downstairs just before midday to find her mother making neat stacks of towels and bed linen and napery on the kitchen table. Liv recognised these as the second-string supplies which June had downgraded to the back of the linen press around five years ago.

'Come on, grab a pile,' June said. 'And then I'll give you a hand with your clothes and things.'

Liv followed, bewildered, wondering what use June expected she would have for Battenberg lace table napkins and the embroidered linen hand-towels which used to be laid out in the bathrooms for dinner parties.

In the bungalow, Liv saw that June had been busy that morning populating the kitchen cupboards with crockery and cutlery, cooking utensils and a set of brand new pots. Liv's culinary experience extended to cooking macaroni cheese once or twice, but June had thought of that and placed a spiral-bound copy of the *Central Cookery Book* on the bench near the kettle. In the pantry was plain and self-raising flour in labelled tubs, salt and pepper, brown and white sugar, vinegar and oil.

'That's just to get you started,' June said. 'Your father's set up a direct deposit for you.'

Liv went about opening and closing; there was dishwashing liquid beneath the sink, dishcloths and steel wool still in their plastic wrappings; the kitchen's third drawer was neatly stacked with crisp, pressed tea-towels; there were apples and bananas in a wooden bowl at the end of the bench. Liv was almost afraid to touch these fruits. They gave off energy, radiated with the repressed rage that had put them there, and it was the same with the early flowering camellias that June had snipped from their bushes and set afloat in a wide-mouthed vase on the coffee table. In every cupboard, in every drawer, on every shelf and surface, Liv saw yet another expression of her mother's meticulous, thorough and irreproachably generous severance.

For all of Lauren's life, the bungalow had been there in the view from the windows at the rear of the house. In summer the backdrop for its slate-tiled roof was the ballooning green of the cherry trees in leaf; in winter, it was bare branches and river water. During her days at school, Lauren was preoccupied with her own concerns: the incomprehensibility of chemistry equations, furtive observations of Nick Hanson, how best to deflect viola jokes during string ensemble, how to retouch make-up at lunchtime without getting ticked off for wearing make-up in the first place. She hardly thought of Liv at all. But when she was at home, the bungalow seemed forever in her peripheral vision and she could not help but notice its signs of life. Windows shadowed briefly with Liv's swollen form, curtains opened and closed.

June had talked to Lauren about Liv. There had been conversations on related topics, too: contraception, intimacy, responsibility. In these matters, Lauren knew exactly what was expected of her, but she didn't know how she was supposed to behave towards Liv. She didn't know whether to largely ignore her sister the way her parents seemed to be doing, or whether it had been inexplicitly left to her to bridge the house and the bungalow, to be the one who could convey slices of leftover cake and small pieces of news.

She hovered between the two positions. For days at a time she would steer clear of the bungalow and of Liv, but then she would find that she could not really leave either of them alone—not the bungalow with its stale and unwelcoming smell, nor this new version of her sister, bloated and subdued, who ate all day and had let her violin warp out of tune in its case. So she would venture down there carrying two milkshakes, perhaps, or two plates of honeyed crumpets, and sit for a while with Liv. But it didn't matter whether she went down there, or stayed away, she lived now with the vague, niggling sensation of having been disloyal.

It was June who rang up to make Liv's various appointments, who drove her to them, and paid for them with her credit card. She sat, self-contained, with Liv in the waiting room, and followed—without expressly having been asked—into the consulting room. The doctor anchored his measuring tape to Liv's solar plexus with his thumb, towed it over the mountain of her stomach to the top of her pelvic bone. Liv felt his bare hands pushing on her tummy skin, although it was partly numb from the stretching. She also felt his gloved fingers cramming up inside of her, but not even this hurt or embarrassed her as much as the way her mother sat by the side of the doctor's desk quietly suffering her own shame.

Liv could almost have convinced herself that it was to save her mother and not to punish her that she decided to labour alone. On a morning in midwinter, in the dark before dawn, Liv walked quietly up the side of the house with her overnight bag—the pain stopping her now and then—to the taxi which waited for her in the street. Liv told herself that what she was about to do was nothing new, nothing new at all, and that girls younger than herself had managed it all alone.

She found there was something reassuringly artificial about the hospital at this hour of the day. Perhaps it was only the slightly illicit feeling of being out-of-hours in a busy place; she might have felt the same at a school, or a library or department store. Or perhaps it came from the contrast between the almost-dawn dimness of the street and the bright fluorescent light within, the chemical smell of the denatured air that was being breathed by uniformed people who had clearly been awake all night. This didn't seem to her like a place where anything bad could happen in real life. Waiting at the maternity reception desk, Liv could almost have been in an airport, a hotel, a cinema, a film.

A midwife checked Liv's blood pressure and pulse, timed her contractions with the electronic stopwatch she kept on a rope around her neck.

'You're certain there's no-one we should call?' the midwife asked, and then, when Liv said yes she was certain, left her alone in a room that was grey and white and almost entirely filled by a monstrous bed with thick, metal rails.

Throughout the morning, the pain worsened. For all of her belly's wrenching and squeezing, Liv's body would not open up in the least. Her doctor came by to examine her.

'This is not going quite the way I'd like,' he said. 'Olivia? Olivia? Can we call your mother? I really think it would be best. This is not going to be easy.'

'I can do this,' Liv insisted.

More hours passed and the thumping pain continued with rhythmic regularity. The midwife who came on for the afternoon shift took away Liv's vomit-stained hospital gown, laced her into a fresh one.

'Honey, are you sure there's not a friend, or an aunt, or anyone at all that we can call for you?'

Liv shook her head, no, and she held steady to her course, all the way out to the furthest reaches of her endurance. By the time she began to scream for her mother, it was from deep in a pain that the gas she was sucking could not touch, and by then she had gone beyond her capacity to say the whole of June's mobile number out loud. The telephone in the empty house by the river rang, and rang, and rang.

The baby, too, began to panic, her tiny heart pumping much too fast, but Liv was past comprehension when the doctor explained to her that she would require an emergency caesarean, that there was no time, now, for a spinal block. Liv barely felt the needle as it pierced her skin. But she did feel—deeply, gratefully—the chemical quicksand of anaesthesia as it closed irresistibly over the top of her.

The baby was very small, and very beautiful. Everyone who came to see her remarked on her fair downy hair, admired the contours of her petite nose, put their fingers into her tiny clutches. Everyone wanted to touch her and hold her, and for a few days her perfection was enough; the hospital room filled up with flowers. Liv had only to say the word, *Cleo*, and all of a sudden that was her baby's name and other people were writing down it on hospital charts and forms.

This, then, was a baby. Not a blank thing, after all, Liv discovered. Not an outline to be inked in by parents and teachers and other good influences—not like that at all, but a whole person, ready made. Liv felt Cleo's frustration that she couldn't make full use of it yet: the complete, intact personality that was inside of her, hidden like the mechanism of a music box, but *there* nevertheless. And this was unexpected, too: that Cleo seemed to Liv not a helpless thing, not at all, but a creature full of power.

When Cleo was asleep, deactivated and inert, it was easy for Liv to love the sight of her. She loved her with a hunger that wanted to eat her, to lick her unreasonably perfect brand new skin, to bite her succulent little limbs. But Liv already suspected that in any game of cannibalism, Cleo would win. When Cleo was awake, Liv—sensing the ferocity of her baby's desire to survive, and how impersonal that was—was afraid. Liv knew already that if it was what Cleo had to do, she would consume Liv's identity whole, suck it out of her breasts and shit it into the nappies that Liv herself would fold, and bin, and consign to landfill.

Once Liv and Cleo had come home, Lauren would decide each afternoon, as she walked back from school under the bare branches of the horse chestnuts that lined their street, whether she would go first to the house, or first to the bungalow to visit with her sister and her niece. She liked to think of having a niece. It felt responsible, special, as if she had been chosen to have more than most other girls of her age to deal with.

This day was a Friday, and cold. As she walked, Lauren pushed up the sleeve of her itching school jumper for what must have been the eightieth time since double Chemistry when Nick Hanson had pinned her wrist to the laboratory bench and carved his telephone number in blue biro on the tender skin of her inner arm. The pen had left little clots of

ink at the top and the tail of each numeral, but she had worn
these down by now to smudges and streaks.

Lauren touched her hand to the ink and there it was, still:
the thudding pulse, the blood pooling in unfamiliar parts of
her flesh and her skin. She flushed again at the memory of
the painful, all-over blush she had experienced when Nick's
hand was holding down her wrist, his dark hair just under
her nose and smelling of chlorine and conditioner. It was
the first time he had come near her in nine days, the first
interest of any kind that he had shown in her since early
the previous week when they'd all been down on the bottom
green and the bell had gone for the end of lunch. Everyone
else headed up the hill, but he'd held her back, pulled her
behind the southern wall of the art block and launched at
her with a sloppy, hurried tongue kiss. Then he'd jogged
away, backwards against the slope, still watching her with that
smart-arse grin of his as she stood there with the back of her
hand to her mouth, waiting for him to turn around so that
she could wipe away the wetness.

It wasn't the fact of sex that surprised or confused Lauren.
She understood that feelings like the ones she had when Nick
touched her could easily flood all the way through you and
short-circuit your everyday brain, make you want to do things
that you would normally think were revolting and strange.
She could even imagine, in the vaguest of ways, how her
parents might couple together in their lofty king-sized bed.
What she didn't know was how people managed to get over

the embarrassment and be calm and normal with each other afterwards, how you went from the stickiness and tongues and the aching between the legs to 'Would you like a cup of tea?' and 'Have you seen my striped shirt?'. She couldn't even look at Nick Hanson, couldn't catch sight of him lighting a Bunsen burner or tugging his bag out of his locker, without her cheeks throbbing at the thought of his tongue in her mouth, his spit on her lips.

She knocked on the door of the bungalow, and Liv, in stretched layers of grey jersey, opened it with Cleo in her arms. Lauren asked right away if she could hold the baby, was overcautious as she took hold of Cleo about supporting her head, which felt surprisingly like a ripe grapefruit in her hand. There were video clips playing softly on the television and draped over the headrests of one of the fat lady couches was a pile of clear plastic drycleaning sleeves, each one protecting a garment for a baby or small child. The linen and muslin, the velvet and lace—Lauren recognised them from the photo albums and the occasional time she had insisted on her mother showing her through the wardrobe in one of the spare rooms of the house.

'All our old things,' Lauren said, although most of the things had originally been made for, or belonged to, Liv.

'Mum brought them down. What do you think?' Liv gestured in the manner of a hand model to a long gown with a smocked bodice, grub roses embroidered all around the hem. There was a matching cap with long pink ribbons that tied it, for now, to the neck of the coat hanger. 'Is it perhaps a little over the top for a trip to Kmart?'

'Gorgeous, though,' Lauren said.

Liv let it fall over the arm of the couch. 'I guess you can never get enough of the things you don't really need.'

Cleo was squirming in a way that made Lauren feel unsatisfactory, and to want to hand her back. She had only wanted to hold her for a moment.

'She's hungry,' Liv said, dispassionately. 'She's always hungry. Give her here.'

Liv sat on the floor and lifted her layers of clothing, but the breast Lauren glimpsed before Cleo attached herself to it was not at all like one of her sister's taut, rounded breasts. Instead the flesh looked to have been flattened out. The too-bright nipple was chapped and sticking out at an angle.

For all of Lauren's life, Liv had existed on a separate plane, a place eighteen months beyond her, where more things were permissible, possible, known. But now, she saw, Liv had gone further still. Although Lauren could see Liv, and touch her, the distance between them was now so great that they were barely in the same universe.

'What's it like?' Lauren asked.

Lauren herself didn't know precisely what she meant.

'I'm so scared,' Liv said.

Up in the house, Lauren found that her mother was entertaining. She would have known this from the kitchen alone, which had been left not in its usual state of spotless tidiness, but with a recipe book propped open on a stainless-steel holder, a jar of preserved lemons on the bench beside it, herbs clustered greenly on a chopping board, and a copy of the latest *Notebook* magazine angled artfully by the telephone along with a fabric-covered journal and pen. Lauren supposed that Hattie Bourke and Marion Clovelly, who sat with her mother at the kitchen table, must put on equivalent displays of leisured productivity when June Wishart came to visit them. Surely they no longer fooled each other. And, yet, they persisted.

'How was school, missy?' Hattie asked. 'Did you see Toby about? Anything I should know?'

'No confirmed sightings, Hat,' Lauren said, although she wouldn't have told Hattie a thing in any case. 'Hi, Marion.'

Hattie, Marion and her mother with three lipstick-stained wine glasses and a barely nibbled cake in front of them: the signs of debriefing in progress. Over the years, Lauren had inconspicuously listened as her mother, Hattie and Marion covered husbands, mothers, friends and acquaintances, catastrophes.

Hattie was an athletic woman of about fifty with a no-nonsense bearing that Lauren associated with the fact of her being a mother of sons. She had once been a sportswoman of note and remained fit, but, even so, it could only be down to spectacular genes that she still had the smooth, taut calves and upper arms of a twenty-year-old. For best, she wore short and figure-hugging shift dresses which showed off her flat stomach, but most often she wore sporty clothes and sandshoes and put into her short hair some kind of product that made it look perpetually damp, as if she were always just coming, going, glowing, from the gym. There was nothing the gym could do, though, for the skin of her face, rutted as it was by sun and sauvignon blanc.

'You have to set clear boundaries,' she was saying to June. 'Tell her that you'll have the baby for a few hours every Tuesday morning, or whichever is best for you. If you're not definite in the early days, you'll end up a permanent free babysitting service and, God knows, we've done our time.'

Marion looked and sounded an altogether gentler person. She had a prayer-soft voice and a cloud of fine hair, which she had controversially allowed to grow out into its bright, natural silver. But there was something in the watchful set of her face, the twists at the corners of her mouth, that hinted to Lauren of dangerous disappointments, resentments and judgements.

'I don't think you want to be setting regular days, actually,' Marion said. 'Then they come to expect it and you're locked in. What about when you want to travel? I wouldn't be committing to that sort of thing if I were you. Not at our stage of life.'

Lauren filled the kettle at the kitchen sink. Through the window, she noticed the overflowing garbage bin at the back door of the bungalow and thought how her mother must hate that with company over. Rita Bunting at the top of her staircase was banging on a tin with a spoon, calling belligerently for her cats.

'Julia and Geoff have put their house on the market,' Marion said.

This might have seemed apropos of nothing, but Lauren knew it was entirely relevant. Julia and Geoff had three adult children; the two eldest already had babies and their youngest was about to have her first.

'They're really going to do it?' Hattie asked, impressed.

'As soon as the baby's born, they're off, interstate,' Marion continued. 'Julia says she doesn't care which city so long as none of her grandchildren live in it, and so long as they can find an apartment within walking distance of the GPO.'

Lauren flicked through the pages of the *Notebook* magazine, saw advertisements with slim older women walking, powerfully and inspiringly alone, on beaches.

'Well, good for them,' said Hattie.

The kettle boiled, Lauren poured. The sky was darkening. Down at the bottom of the garden a window of the bungalow shone suddenly, brilliantly, yellow.

'You have to think about illness, too,' Hattie pointed out.

'We're not getting any younger and bugs these days seem to be nastier,' Marion said. 'They can go on forever.'

Lauren ventured to glance over at June. She tried to remember if it had ever before been her mother sitting in the receiving chair, but the only images she could summon showed her mother poised and immaculate, filling wine glasses, fetching tissues. It hurt Lauren to watch the way her mother grasped at every scrap of advice Hattie and Marion gave to her, making fervid, grateful little nods, as if she were now too impoverished to refuse anything that was offered. June looked as if she were in the dock, cowed and diminished, guilty. Lauren took her cup of tea to the table, nudged her mother to make room, wedged in beside her on the same chair, although there were plenty of others. Sitting so close, Lauren could feel the shudder in her mother's breathing, see the tears inside her eyelids.

'Don't you ever do this to me, will you?' June took Lauren's hand and gave it a squeeze, and Lauren felt something inside of herself expand. She squeezed back. A promise. And later that night, in the bathroom on the top floor of the house that Lauren no longer had to share with anyone, she stood in the shower and scrubbed away Nick Hanson's phone number with a nailbrush. She scrubbed and scrubbed until her skin was red and it hurt.

⌘

In the first weeks of Cleo's life, Liv learned why infants were put into Baby Björns: it was to keep mothers in their places. Cleo entered every room first, absorbed every first greeting, every first kiss, Liv trailing her as inevitably as a caboose. Liv knew that she had been eclipsed, perhaps forever, but it was strange to Liv how little she minded. Out of all the things Cleo had stolen from her, sleep was really the only one she resented. Cleo woke at night only about as much as a new baby should, but the hours between the night-time feeds tortured Liv.

Sometimes she got up out of bed and squeezed herself into the corner of one of the fat lady couches as if hoping to be consumed by its folds and creases. Often, she would turn on the television, but rarely the light. This made her eyes feel gritty and she had a sense of the synthetic brightness of the screen sucking at the moisture in her skin. From her living room Liv could see the rear of the Bunting place and there were nights when she was sure Rita Bunting, her top-storey windows flickering with pulsing light, was watching the same channel.

Liv knew she should at least try to sleep, and so there were nights when she didn't get up, only lay there in the too-soft double bed with her eyes closed, fighting herself for comfort and release. She counted, imagined lying down in a warm meadow with sheep. She towed her mind, meditatively, through the muscles of her body from toes to scalp, but always her thoughts would crash through any fragile peace she could conjure, and the thoughts she had after midnight were the ugliest of all.

There were snatches of sleep, though, and during these she would catch a glimpse of a dream, always the same one. It was of a hotel with limitless corridors and mirrored elevators but, although its plush burgundy arteries seemed infinite, there was never enough time for Liv to get anywhere inside of them before she woke in the dark to mewling sounds she was not even certain she had heard. She would lurch out of bed, trying not to bruise her thighs on the furniture or open the bedroom door into her face. Still half-lost in the hotel, she would think at first—wish and hope—that the small, crying baby in the next room was the illusion made of dream-stuff, and not those long, velvety corridors of promise.

A few of Liv's friends came to the bungalow to see her. She could tell they had enjoyed their time at a children's wear boutique, picking out a small skirt with frills or a hat with ears, but she knew the real reason they had come was to safely observe the thing from which, by luck or good management, they themselves had been delivered. June's friends came in greater numbers, bringing with them tubs of pumpkin soup and hand-me-downs, holding Cleo for a while and then handing her back without failing to tell Liv how wonderful it was to be able to do so. They had been through their garages and lofts and found books and puzzles and games, high chairs and portable cots. Hattie Bourke brought a stately pram with a broad navy-blue canopy and white wheels and tyres, which Hattie had taken to with a tube of sandshoe whitener.

'It's not really *in*,' Hattie said. 'But it was the best you could buy when the boys were little.'

It wasn't the sort of pram you could easily fold up and put in a car, but one for relaxed mothers who strolled around the streets of their own neighbourhoods. Fitted with a firm mattress, it would only do for a few months until Cleo was ready to sit up.

'I'll have it back when you're done with it,' Hattie said in her forthright way, and Liv understood that she was thinking of her own grandchildren, even as she held little Cleo in her arms.

It was a boastful sort of pram, Liv thought, as unnecessarily showy and large as a Volvo station wagon. But even if she didn't like it, she began to use it every day. Tucking Cleo under layers of blankets against the cold, Liv set out for her walks without destination or purpose. Soothed by the sense of forward momentum, she walked sometimes towards the city, sometimes away from it, taking shelter in cafés or under shade sails when it rained.

'I am surprising people,' Liv told Babs, on the phone.

Babs planned to fly south to meet Cleo later in the year, towards the end of spring when the weather improved.

'They say I am managing beautifully.'

She knew they watched how she put the baby dextrously to her breast. Did it remind them of the way she once put her violin to her chin? They watched, too, the way she now swung the baby up out of her cot, instinctively nestling Cleo's head into the crook of her arm. She was surprised, herself, to learn how swiftly the body memorised new actions.

'I bet they go back up to the house and tell June that this baby just might be the making of me,' Liv said.

And if they did, Liv thought, it was only because they didn't know what she thought about in the night when she wasn't sleeping. They didn't know about her plans, and that was because nobody could ever know. She wasn't sure if she would ever go through with any one of the plans, but if she ever told the least thing, the door to all of them would be forever closed.

She thought about drowning. Sitting Cleo up in the bath water in that inflatable chair that someone had given her, and then ducking out to answer the phone. Everyone would call her stupid, and negligent, but not evil, and surely intention was all? It might be easier just to drop her hairdryer in the water.

Liv knew her small city's waterfront by heart, and in the dark of a sleepless night could map out all of the many places where one might reasonably trip. She would have to be sure to do up the single strap, the one that went around the baby's middle and over the top of her blankets, or else the baby might float up and out of the sinking pram.

And yet, in the light of the day, if she bumped Cleo's head by accident on the doorframe, Liv would almost cry out of sorrow and remorse. On the day she took Cleo to the GP to be immunised, Liv watched her baby's face crumple with the shock of the first needle, and then, as the GP readied the second one, Liv screamed out, 'Don't. Please don't hurt her. Don't hurt her any more.'

𝒟

More weeks passed. Cleo grew, and still Liv did not sleep. Or, to be truthful, she slept like a starving person ate, each day finding just enough to keep from dying, but nothing more. The sleeplessness left her shaky and nauseated, perpetually afraid. Although she tried to get out of the bungalow for a small part of each day, every aspect of journeying into the outside world cost energy she had not been able to store. Walking the streets with Cleo in the pram, Liv found she had developed a habit of walking close to walls, just in case she suddenly needed their support.

But sleep, it turned out, was a tidal wave. All the sleepless days and weeks, and the months they had become: these were only the long, slow out-suck. When sleep came rushing back to Liv, it was with the kind of momentum that could uproot trees, move entire houses, tear an infant from its mother's grip.

She had been in town for most of the morning. She had visited the library, where she had sat with Cleo among the big, bright beanbags, letting her chew the corners of board books. She had also been to a café, where she ordered a cappuccino and sat in a booth seat, concealed from street view, to breastfeed her baby. The café was at the top end of a block in one of the city's steeper thoroughfares, and Liv had just pushed the pram back out through the door onto the street. It was early spring: one of those gusty equinoctial days when the sky suddenly thickens, colours itself a dirty orange, violet and blue. She was standing on the pavement in a cold wind. Nobody would have been surprised if it had snowed that day. Some of the kinder people even suggested that maybe the weather had played a part.

The pram looked almost jolly as it capered away down the slope. You could imagine the jaunty kind of music that would have accompanied it in a silent film. There was only a single pedestrian on that side of the street at the time and, when he saw the pram coming, he stepped considerately out of its way. Later, once the story was all over the news, he would wonder how it was possible that he had been so absorbed—his mobile phone close and hot on his ear—that he had failed to properly register what it was that rollicked towards him down the gradient of the pavement. He might easily have caught it, but it rolled straight past him, down towards the intersection where stopped cars waited for the green light that came at the split second the pram hopped the curb and trundled out onto the road. Baby Cleo, if she had looked the right way, would have seen a shield wall of gleaming chrome.

By the following day almost everyone had an opinion. Of the people who knew Liv, some shook their heads and said that she had always been the unstable one out of those two girls; you only had think back to her eighteenth birthday party. But others said what happened at the party was just a bit of a laugh. For goodness sake, she was young and beautiful and talented—a little wild along with it, maybe, but not the sort to harm her own child.

Every few hours in those early days after the accident, Lauren would find herself drawn to the computer screen, looking for answers in the places she had been trained to find them. On every site that her searches uncovered, the pictures were exactly the same: there was the misshapen pram, the woman driver with her big, black sunglasses and her hands over her mouth, the paramedics on their knees in the street with their masks and tubes and fold-out toolboxes. Between their bodies were glimpses of terry towelling, cotton, skin.

Beneath the pictures were the reports—the same scant details worked through in slightly different phrasing—and, beneath those, there were chat threads that went on for pages. Sceptics said Liv had staged the whole thing, childless women said she hadn't deserved her precious gift, religious people said it was God's will, ordinary people said poor little thing. There were calls for compassion, for censure, for wrist straps to be compulsory on prams. The only thing that everyone could all agree on was that Liv let go of the pram. As she fell to the ground, the fingers of both her hands uncurled, her thumbs unhooked. And the pram, baby tucked snugly within, careered into the late-morning traffic.

It's a hospital bed and yet it might easily be a bier, high and white and marble. Someone skilled enough could make out of stone the kinds of clefts and rumples and creases with which the white sheets mark out the edges of her motionless body. Ignore the tubes that fed her, and the ones that take her waste away, she could easily be a dead princess: her long hair loose and brushed into waves that roll down, around and over shoulders and arms that have not yet moved, not even twitched. Her eyeballs beneath their lids do not flicker or shudder; and, although she is breathing, if anyone said they saw her breast rise or fall, they would be lying, even if out of the best of possible motives. Soon, it will be four months.

In the early weeks, June came every day to the hospital, although there were days when she didn't make it past the lobby downstairs. Often, Lauren would find her standing there, between the vending machines and the elevators and comfortable chairs: just standing there, as still as all the other pillars holding the ceiling and the floor apart, caught—bewildered—between her daughter on the first floor above, and her granddaughter in the mortuary below. After five weeks of waiting for Liv to wake up, to bear witness, they buried Cleo anyway. They put her in the gown embroidered with grub roses at the hem, found that the matching cap was useful for covering up the worst of the damage to her skull.

Most often, now, it's Lauren who sits with Liv, watching for signs of change. Sometimes she's there when two nurses come with a gurney and a long, flat plastic board. They tip Liv sideways and slide the board underneath her, use it to lift her onto the gurney where she lies while they change the sheets on her bed. Afterwards they settle her back in, smooth the sheets around her, but it's Lauren who brushes her hair so it falls just so, and Lauren who burns the scented oils, changes the CDs in the player.

A nurse hums along without appearing to know the tune of the *Duo for Violin and Viola in B flat major.* As she hums, she checks the drip, the tubes, the heavy plastic bag hanging by the bed.

'I suppose you wonder, too,' she says to Lauren, 'what she's dreaming about.'

But Lauren can see no signs of dreaming at all. Liv shows to the world no soft sighs, no winces of grief. Nor any secret smiles.

If Lauren were able to fit into the rabbit hole of Liv's ear, to fall through the dark swerving tunnels, tumble past the hammering of tiny and intricate bones, crawl through the soft curling ram horns of brain, right down into the centre, then she would know that Liv is dreaming. She is dreaming of sleep, and in her dream sleep she is also dreaming, and in that dream, she dreams of being asleep. She sleeps and dreams without any intention to wake, sleeping as if between two mirrors that shrink her dreams in endless recursion to the prick of a pin: a pin upon whose head dance infinite angels, each one of them whispering 'sleep'.

nag

The wagon rests in winter, the sleigh in summer, the horse never.

I REMEMBER HOW I rested my cheek against the seat back and gave myself up to the rattle and the hum. One stockinged foot tucked beneath me, the sole of the other flat to the vibrating floor and I was on my way. Speeding down the straights, slowing for the curves: I felt it all and might almost have swayed with the motion, except that—for now—it was only the sewing machine in the corner of the front room on a cold night in May and my mother working the treadle with a lapful of cotton, finishing off my dress on our last night together. It was 1958.

I didn't want to cause her any hurt, and I wouldn't, I thought, just so long as I kept from smiling on the outside of my face and just so long as I didn't lean in to the bends. That way there would be no need for my mother to be sad, or even to know, that in my heart I was already on tomorrow's train, upright through two days and a night with the other girls, all of us speeding west, away into new lives. I looked over at my mother where she sat in the yellow flood of the standing lamp, a row of pins in her mouth like a half crown of thorns.

I don't suppose my mother had any way of knowing, when I was born—the last of her children—how gently she might have handled me and yet still have me turn out the same. She'd been trained on my brothers, six of them in all, and so, at long last when I came along, she was already, what you might call, a bit hard in the mouth. Another woman might have given up after three sons, or four, but my mother wanted her girl. Nanna said, as a child, my mother would spend hours dressing her doll, changing its name every time she changed her mind about what she would call a daughter once she had one of her own. I have that doll still—her china fingers chipped, her scalp covered with hard dots of glue and matted wisps of her once glorious chestnut hair—although I don't know if she was ever called Stella, like me.

It is a responsibility to be wanted in that way, and I sometimes wonder if it was the depths of my mother's wanting that moulded in me the heights of my eagerness to please her. I think this is what must have happened before I was born, because I came out that way, a pleaser—just the fact I was a girl was evidence enough of that. My mother wanted to be a nurse. When I told my father I was to start my training, he said, 'Nurses are whores', without looking up from his paper. I know my mother would have liked a starched white veil and a watch pinned to her breast and to walk in white shoes the length of a corridor knowing that all was right in the ward because she had made it so. Of course it was always going to be my mother who put the idea of nursing into my head, but it wasn't anonymously the way she thought. Perhaps when I was younger she had sneaked all kinds of thoughts of her own like cuckoo eggs into my mind but, by the time I decided to go nursing, I was much too old for that.

On our last night together, I had already been living away from home for the two years of my training and my mother hadn't minded. The boarding house by the hospital was not so very far from our house by tram, and my mother knew that if Matron and the landlady between them could not keep me out of trouble, then the punishing hours of a trainee nurse would do the job. My mother had never imagined, though, that when my training was complete, I might take a job so very far away: on the other side of the country which was also the other side of the world for all the difference it made, the distance was so great.

The whirring of the sewing machine was a purring in my blood. Backwards, forwards, backwards, forwards. Snip. The seam was done and my mother looked at it critically before turning the dress right side out, shaking out its gathers, picking at some loose threads. And now I could smile, at the dress supposedly. The fabric was a soft green with bunches of large blue flowers of a kind that I'd never seen grown in a garden.

'Let's have a look at you, then,' my mother said, and I put aside the crochet blanket and stood in my bra and petticoats in front of the empty fireplace. That fireplace was like a small black mouth turned downwards at the corners but, although I was cold, I didn't complain. The fabric had come at the cost of the coal. My mother bunched up the dress and pulled it down over me; she pinched and primped and pinned, but I knew how to stand so the points of the pins didn't prick.

My mother stood back then, and looked at me hard. For all of that night I had been waiting for her to say something, but so far there had been nothing, or at least nothing of the sort I had been expecting. Perhaps it was coming now. A sermon could not go for nineteen years, surely, without its conclusion, without one final flourish to pull together its themes? And if not a culmination, then there ought at the very least, I thought, to be a summary, one last run through of just the most important points. But which would they be?

I had the whole thing by heart, chapter and verse (*on no account spend more than you earn, frugality is freedom, avoid men who drink, do not drink yourself because women who drink are vulgar, avoid men who gamble, gambling is a sign of degeneracy, waste not: want not, a lady does not discuss politics, religion or money, people with thin lips are invariably cruel, turn the other cheek, practise the Golden Rule, never leave a party before the guest of honour, a lady is known by her fingernails and her shoes, bright lipstick is vulgar, never brush your hair in public, there is nothing attractive about a skirt worn above the knee, marry wisely and not for love, and not exactly for money either, but make no mistake about it that marriage is a business, mend your clothes before you hang them on the line and not afterwards, never be seen eating or smoking in the street, a pair of rabbits will feed you for a week if you are careful* with them, but you—yes, you—with all the opportunities you've had, let's hope you never have to be as careful as I have had to be . . . and so on) and yet there was a part me that wanted to know which parts would, on a night like this one, be uppermost on my mother's mind.

Still she said nothing, not even when she was looking at my face instead of at the dress which she'd made to be just like I was, full in the chest and nipped at the waist, flat in the belly but flared in the hips. This was to be the best of my four dresses: I'd wear a third petticoat beneath it for dancing.

'Righto, lovey. Hem,' she said. So I got up in my stockinged feet onto a straight-backed chair and turned slowly around while she fussed and folded and pinned. I put my arms out like a ballerina.

'Down you get,' she said, when she was done. 'And make me a cup of tea, will you?'

Even the air in the kitchen felt full of the fact of my leaving, its motes thicker or more numerous, slowing me down as I boiled the kettle and made tea. I remember how I reached down that yellow cup, its fellows all lined up perfectly on the middle shelf of the dresser, each one upside down on its saucer. I remember how carefully I noticed the cool of the lemon yellow glaze against my fingertips, how I watched the milk detonating deep in the dark water of the tea (*girls with class put their milk in last*). Where was my father that night? Not in the kitchen. Maybe my mother and I were up late to finish the dress. Perhaps he'd already gone to bed.

I set my mother's cup on the sideboard. She'd pushed her chair away from the sewing machine and was doing the hem by hand. It must have been late, and she must have been tired, because why else would the needle have slipped and gone into her fingertip? She made a little yip of pain and I saw the dark red of her blood, a blob of it like an upside-down drip from a tap, a swelling droplet almost ready to fall. But that wasn't what made me rush at her, to go down on my knees the way I did. What made me do that was the pained way her face was shaping up, when I knew perfectly well that the needle's prick wasn't enough to hurt her—not a woman like my mother who'd given birth seven times and chopped off the top of her left little finger with a meat cleaver that time my second oldest brother banged into her as she was quartering a chook.

There was only one other time in my whole life that I'd seen my mother cry and that was when Nanna died. She hadn't done it when the phone call came from the hospital, or even at the church or the graveyard afterwards. She waited until we'd washed up all the cups and saucers and the big oval plates that had held the sandwiches. Three of my brothers were still at home then, and she waited until all of us children had gone to bed, and then she sat down in the front room with a hanky. I heard her from my bedroom and I came to the doorway of the front room with the intent to comfort her, but the sight of her hunched over and heaving by the fireplace—her mouth all out of shape with the middle of her top lip curving down into the cave of her mouth—frightened me back to bed.

Now she cradled her stuck hand high to her chest. In the corner of her eye there was a tear and it looked big as a whole world, but I had a hanky tucked inside my bra. Of course I did. I was my mother's daughter and the hanky was fine and small and white with a small lacy square of crochet in one corner and a picot edging all around. I pulled it out, quick as a coward surrendering, although I hardly knew where to aim it. She looked at me then with that strange, terrible downwards curve to her mouth and I was glad when she took the hanky and pressed it to her eyes, then sobbed through her nose so that the horrible mouth closed. And even then she didn't say anything, but after a while folded up the hanky and gave it back to me, damp, with a little red smudge on the lacework.

I wish I had a photo, or better yet that I could take you there. On the platform, I'd have you stand up on tippy toes and press your nose against the round-shouldered windows and watch us as we walked down the tunnel of the train, looking for somewhere to sit all together, the four of us. There I am in the dress my mother had hemmed the night before, and my hair was dark like yours is now: thick and matte, near black, with a wave. It was good hair, except for how quickly it got greasy between washes. That day I'd pulled it into a bun, used a tiny brush to make an extra margin around my lips in a shade called Sky Blue Pink.

We were going so far west that we would cross almost the entire country. Isabel and Kitty would get off first; they were going to a mining town that was dirt-red, famous and full of men. Reggie and I were heading further still, to a district hospital in the farming country on the desert's other side. On the platform were all our mothers, some sisters and a little brother or two, but not our fathers; it must have been a weekday, the day we went away. But look at us, the four of us, at our serious gestures, the way we hold our elbows in tight to our bodies as if we're out for tea in company. Frowning and offering suggestions, pointing with gloved hands, taking careful steps in our heels, keeping in check arms and legs that have only just lately been tamed down from cartwheels and handstands. We're working so hard at being grown-up that we're even convincing ourselves, and yet, look: all you'd have to do is smirk or tickle any one of us and we'd giggle, give ourselves away as the oversized girls that we are.

Only a month earlier we'd been plain-faced and in our uniforms—blue dresses, white caps—standing in the corridor outside Matron's room, waiting. We'd shined our brown shoes, checked for each other that the seams of our flesh-coloured tights were dead straight up the backs of our calves.

'Avery,' called Matron and it was as if a gun had gone off, I jumped that quick away from the wall.

Matron's room was small and windowless but she'd set out a doily on her desk with a little glass vase and a posy of the marguerite daisies I recognised from the park that we all ran through every morning on our way from the boarding house, still sticking pins in our buns as we went. I never knew if it was the same for the other three still outside in the corridor, but I saw a different part of Matron that day. I felt that she let me see it, too, quite deliberately. It was as if there was a ripped seam down the wide, white side of her uniform, from armpit to hip, and that she herself held the stitches apart for me to get a look at the soft stuff within.

Matron wished me well for my future and handed over a letter she had written. It was in an unsealed envelope and she nodded that I should open it, clearly pleased with herself, as if it were a gift she had taken time and care in choosing. I didn't see all the words, but I saw the important ones like *eager* and *willing* and *diligent*, each one of them a big, fat, blue rosette I could take home and pin to my proud mother's chest.

Matron told me, as she'd tell the others waiting outside, about the vacancies over in the west. 'A little adventure might be good for you. You especially,' she said, and I wished even then I'd had the courage to ask her what she meant rather than stand there guessing. 'Don't you think?' she asked. 'Hmm?'

But the thing was that I'd never yet thought of my own life as a thing whose shape and dimensions were within my own control, and if you asked me how my own life seemed to me at the time, then I'd probably have thought of a white apron or one of Nanna's best vases or some other thing that I was supposed not to mess up or allow to fall.

'Thank you, Matron.'

For all of the time we'd been at the hospital, we'd been obedient to the rule that you didn't address Matron unless you were spoken to first. And, although this was my chance, the thoughts going around in my head wouldn't neaten themselves up into questions I could ask without seeming rude. I wanted to ask her if her hand felt bare without a ring there, if it was enough that the children in the pictures on her desk were nieces and nephews. I felt I ought to confess to her about how my father said nurses were whores. She looked, to me, like a nun.

✿

I'd stand there with you if I could, at the window of that train. I'd like to see Reggie again, the way she was then: fair as I was dark and with her hair styled in smooth coils on either side of her face. Perhaps if I could see that face again now, I'd be able to tell exactly what it was about Reggie that used to make my mother go all tight and disapproving when I brought her home for tea. Maybe it was nothing more than the too-good-to-be-true dolly sweetness of the large blue eyes or the way she painted her top lip into sharp little points in Schoolhouse Red.

Reggie's mother made all of her clothes just the way my mother made mine, but Reggie had all the latest things straight away.

'But look at them close up,' my mother used to say. 'No finish. No polish.'

The thing was, though, that Reggie was always onto the next frock before the slightly skewed zip or the unfelled hem could even begin to matter.

'Just watch out for that one,' my mother used to say.

And I'd say, 'Oh, Ma.'

What I knew about Reggie was that she was clever in a quick way that had nothing to do with the inside of a schoolbook. It showed up in a kind of forethought that would have come in handy to her on a chessboard, not that any of us knew the least thing, then, about queens and knights and pawns. Reggie seemed always to know what was about to happen long before I did, and where to put herself to best advantage. We'd both been there in the ward when a baby, just a few days old, died for no good reason anyone could see, but I only stood there and gawped. I just stood there looking at the weeping mother sitting on the high bed, still holding a shape to her breast even though Sister had taken the baby away and laid it on its back in its cot where she was swaddling it tight in white sheeting.

I never even saw Reggie move, but when Sister turned around, Reggie was over the other side of the bed by the mother and it was me standing there with an empty look that needed filling with the job no-one wanted to do. Meanwhile Reggie got to make the mother a cup of tea and try to soothe her down. Two weeks later, when the mother sent Reggie a bottle of gin and a whole carton of Craven A cigarettes, I was still waking in the night from dreams in which I was treading the endless black and white chequered corridors to the hospital morgue with the weight of that dead baby in my arms.

And look again at the four of us, there on the train: Kitty, Isabel, Reggie and me. We've found a table to sit around, two of us facing forward, two facing back, and the old suitcases we've borrowed or been given are stowed in the luggage racks above our heads. But look where Reggie's sitting. She's got the window seat, and it's not the one facing backwards either.

☙

The train came alive underneath and all around us, and it was Reggie who worked out how to unclip the windows and slide them open to the small extent that they'd go. Doors were shutting and whistles being blown and I watched my mother where she stood there in that line of mothers. I saw her reach out as if to stop the train, and then draw her arm back and tuck it under the dark green strap of her handbag. Then the train gave itself a great grinding heave out of stillness into motion. And Isabel had her hanky out, waving it madly.

'Hanky, hanky. Quick, Stel, give us yours,' said Reggie, who never had one of her own when she needed it.

'Get your own rotten hanky,' I said, but she saw the picot edge just peeking out of the sweetheart neckline of my new dress. All in fun, I clutched at it, but too slow—she had nimble-fingered my little lacy hanky away from me and swept it out beyond the glass. I could see it streaming away from her fingers in the rushing air, and I saw how the bright red on the lace had dulled to the colour of rust. I also saw how Reggie's arm, the whole length of it, was on the wrong side of the body of the train. *And what do you think will happen if a train comes the other way? Hmm? Bang, gone, no more arm.*

'Pull your arm in, Reg,' I said.

'Yes, mother,' she said.

And I think it was just the train's gathering speed, or a sudden gust of wind—or perhaps the two together; I don't think Reggie meant for it to happen, but in any case the hanky got free of her grip, snapped open for the briefest of moments—a tiny lace-quartered parachute in an updraft—and was gone.

Six weeks after that my mother died. She'd been standing on a stool putting the kitchen curtains back up after having them down in the wash. The doctor told my brothers that a blood vessel had burst in her brain, that it would have been fairly quick, and that there was nothing anyone could have done even if they'd been there when she fell. I suppose I could have gone home for the funeral but it would have been two days and a night there on the train, and the same back again, and with no mother to see at the other end anyway.

Our new Matron let me have two days off work, although I'd probably have been better off up and about in my uniform than staying back at the boarding house, pacing the parlour like an orphaned kitten. Perhaps I was lucky that an old local lady called Mrs Cowan died at about the same time. She'd turned one hundred the year before and had had a letter from the queen, and we nursed her in the hospital for two weeks while her lungs filled slowly with fluid for the very last time. I went to her funeral and sat in the second row at the church and the family was kind about the terrible way that I cried.

D

Before I lived in Kirby, I'd never stopped to think that farmers might be as vain as anybody else, or that grown men might bitch among themselves like a dorm full of first-year nurses. But it didn't take me long to learn that farmers put their best fences in full view of the passing traffic, and sow their crops most neatly there as well. How straight and strong is a fence, how high is a crop, how fat a mob of sheep—these are the things that tell you who's who in a district, and around here it's always been the Kingsmiths who've had the best of everything.

I know my mother would have liked to see me married to Teddy Kingsmith. The eldest of those three boys, he was tall and well-dressed, and I know she'd have liked his full lips and the way he said please and thank you. She'd have asked for a picture of the Kingsmith place—red bricked and two storeyed and built close to the road even though that family had more land than anybody to choose from—and she'd have put it on the mantelpiece like a trophy.

The first we saw of Teddy Kingsmith was in the hospital after he'd been smashed up in a truck accident while he was away on National Service. They'd put his plaster on down in the city, right up to the hip on one side of his body and as far as the shoulder on the other, then sent him back to Kirby to be close to his family while he healed. It was me who he liked first. I'll never forget the big gap-toothed grin he gave—to me especially, or so it seemed—on the afternoon that he galloped up and down the corridors on his crutches, stiff-legged as a giraffe let loose on the field at Flemington, and the doctor said yes, alright, he could go home.

The next town along the highway from Kirby was Pickering and by city standards it was half a lifetime away, but the country kids just got in their cars and drove—to dances, debates and plays, to football games in the winter, cricket in the summer. When I think of that time, I think of Teddy's Holden ute and how many people you could get in the back if you really tried, the girls with scarves tied down tight over their ears and hair. There was a day we drove all that way to go to a Junior Farmers event where a serious-looking girl with oversized spectacles gave a pancake-making demonstration, as if I needed anybody to show me how to make a well in the flour and patiently work in the egg.

'Don't try to do it too fast,' the girl said, and my mother in my head said, *haste makes waste.*

Reggie rolled her eyes beside me, then got up and went outside for a smoke, but I don't think that it was actually her who said it, afterwards as we stood around in the fading light outside the Pickering Town Hall. I think it was someone else who said, in that lighthearted way that's only half a heartbeat

from dead serious, that it wasn't fair: I'd got to ride all the
way there in the cab of the ute alongside Teddy, they said,
and now it was someone else's turn on the way home. And,
although it was almost dark, there was no mistaking who it was
standing there with her hip already resting on the passenger
side door of the ute. He proposed to her a few months later.

If ever we girls thought we were bold and brave and different,
if ever we fancied ourselves blue stockings—well, we weren't
any of those things. Within twelve months of us getting on
that train, all four of us had rings on our fingers. Your father
and I barely knew each other and yet we partnered up for life
as if it were nothing more serious than the foxtrot and the
music had already begun.

You asked me the last time you came home what I saw in
your father back then, and I suppose I could say that he was
good-looking enough, although somewhat on the short side.
I could say that his hands were firm and dry when he took
hold of mine on the dance floor and that there was something
endearing about the way his hair stuck up in the middle of
the back of his head where he couldn't see to brush it. Maybe
I thought his silences and those darkest-brown eyes were signs
of hidden depths.

I think he thought I was pretty. I think he thought I'd
do. He was twenty-two years old and starting to look about
for a wife and I came to him like a lost banknote on a windy

street: a windfall that he quite reasonably thought he might as well put in his wallet as throw back on the ground. There was nothing much more to it than that. If ever I thought that he would love me passionately, then I had to settle for steadily, and oftentimes I've suspected—and been anywhere from comforted to outraged by the thought—that if you cut my head off and stuck someone else's in its place, Colin would neither notice nor love me the less.

Your father and I set our wedding date three times because it turned out the first two times that the Saturdays we had chosen were already claimed by other couples. It was the season for marriage—after harvest, before seeding—and in the end the wedding was so late that a honeymoon was out of the question. My family never came to the wedding, although my eldest brother's wife went through my mother's possessions as soon as we announced our engagement, picking out things she thought I'd be wanting and putting them in a trunk that crossed the country just the way I had, two days and a night on the train. There were plates and cups and one of Nanna's best vases, tablecloths, quilts and my mother's doll. But right on top, so as I'd find it as soon as I opened the lid, was a brown paper parcel full of cut out pieces of ivory satin and French lace. It was left to me to stitch them together into a dress that was nothing like as beautiful as it was supposed to be.

Our engagement happened so quickly that it had already been decided on before he took me for the first time to the farm. That happened on a day in midsummer and I'd never

been so far from Kirby along the northern road; our socialising never took us out that way. The Palfrey place wasn't a
small holding, but with the rocky paddocks on the eastern
boundary and the salt pans spreading out on either side of
the ditch where the river used to run, the land was hardly
strong. As Colin drove, my eyes took in the unspooling
miles of fences so old and sagging that they'd barely keep in
a determined lamb. I saw the rusting water tanks and listing
windmills, the old weatherboard farmhouse capsizing into
the earth, but I didn't mind any of it, really. I suppose I was
too young to see the hours and dollars that it would take if
you set your heart to fixing it all to perfect, but I also thought
all that brokenness quite pretty.

Mr and Mrs Palfrey had been married a long time and
Colin was a surprise, born late. I wonder if it was just all
the years they'd had together that made them seem more
like siblings than husband and wife. They were both fairly
short, with narrow bones and bird-sharp faces. They had
accents from the north of England and there was something
downcast and resigned in their manner that made me think of
them standing in queues. They had a particular wordless way
of being together, silently and presciently handing between
themselves things like plates and cutlery and spectacles. After
the tea, Colin went with his father to the sheds, leaving his
mother and I to get acquainted.

'So, you're going to marry him?' she said, as if there was
still a chance I might not.

She walked me around on the cushiony green of her couch grass lawn out the front of the big house, showed me her lilac and her roses. The big house was as ugly as it is now—as graceless and as grey—but her garden was beautiful. She'd made it grow in a thin layer of shade cast by the gum trees your great-grandfather planted out even before he'd dug the foundations. She offered to take me down to the cottage, which is where Colin, she supposed, would live. If ever he took on a wife.

The cottage had been built as a place for farm workers so nobody had thought to circle it with trees. Mrs Palfrey went ahead of me and the sun flaming down on us was so hot that it seemed to be making a noise; there was no point trying to talk over it. Small, sticky flies formed and re-formed patterns on the back of her shirt and I flapped at my face, having yet to learn how to avoid breathing them in.

His mother said not to expect flowers. Around the cottage was a fenced yard that separated nothing from nothing else. The baking dirt within and without was equally barren, and the wires were either slack or curling away from their posts, broken. Thorny bushes clung to the dust-stained bricks of the cottage and its outhouse, but even these were stripped of their leaves to the height a sheep could reach.

'I'll leave you to have a look about,' she said. She seemed tired, but I supposed she rarely had visitors.

And now I was alone I could do all the things I wanted, like open up the cupboards and drawers, stand at the kitchen sink and look through the window, imagine my children in that frame.

Half the yard was taken up with the clothesline, a huge metal thing with levers and titling arms and great long stretches of wire. Before long, I'd know that thing better than I knew myself, but on that day it looked to me like a semaphore station or some other sort of machine for sending signals across the pale, dry acres of wheat and sheep all around. It wasn't until we were driving away that Colin told me the water he and I would use to cook, to wash our clothes and dishes and selves, was the water his mother would no longer have for her garden. For her, I was neither a pleasure nor a boon. She was getting me at the expense of her roses.

⌇

I did see the horse that day at the farm, but from far enough away that his pale grey coat showed white against the orange of the soil. I never actually saw him move, but clearly he did because each time I looked out from where we sat with our tea cups on the front veranda, he was standing—quite still—against a different part of fence that ran between the big house and the road. Later, I learned that he was called Lad, that he was old, and now had no particular use. Although he'd been shut out of Mrs Palfrey's flower garden, he had free run of the rest of the home paddock that in those days took in the big house, the cottage and the sheds. Noon would find him pressed up against the side of one or the other of those buildings in whatever narrow stripe of shade that remained. Or else he'd be down at the edge of the home dam, up to his hocks in the silt. They kept him out of sentiment and loyalty—the horse had been Colin's boyhood show pony—and all it cost was a bucket of chaff each day and the occasional inconvenience of horse dung on the paths.

The horse never spoke to me until after the wedding. When I'd seen him only at a distance, my eye had automatically filled the pale contours of his frame with firm flesh, sleeked his coat and thickened his mane and tail, but once I saw him up close, I understood that he was ancient. His pale grey coat had shagged into clumps and he had become so thin, his skin so sucked in against his skeleton, that he was a lesson to me in anatomy. On either side of the tail end of his spine were hollows, the sagging skin propped up again on the lower side by diagonal bones that in all my life of looking at horses I had never imagined to exist there beneath the big, smooth curves of their haunches. From inside the cottage, I sometimes saw the ridge of the horse's back drifting through the frames of my window like the peaks of a dirty iceberg. Or I'd step out the back door to find him rubbing the side of his head against the dusty poles of the clothesline, making an orange streak on his already grubby pelt.

My mother-in-law never sought me out. I'd imagined I would do things like bake cakes and walk them up to her at the big house, but, although I waited for the drapes there to open, they rarely did. In summer she kept them drawn against the sun, and in winter against the cold. And, besides, the pathway to her door would have taken me past those shameful, shrivelling roses. I came to think that the best way to earn her approval was to keep cheerfully and self-sufficiently to myself, so I kept house and made meals and in the busy times, which seemed to go for ten months of the year, more than half those meals were packed into a picnic basket. If I wanted to see my husband, I'd eat sandwiches alongside him while he circled the paddocks in one machine after the other as the seasons went by.

At the cottage there was no cat, and the dog—a kelpie bitch who in any case barely flinched her eyes from Colin's face when I called her name—went out at dawn with Colin into whichever one of the vast flat paddocks needed him that day. He and the dog returned together after dark, and it wasn't unusual for Colin to fall into bed in his clothes. Mr Palfrey's hens sometimes scratched with their big yellow feet in the cottage yard, but they were ugly, flighty birds with small, barely feathered heads and they would take fright and scatter, kicking up dust, if ever I disturbed them at peck.

I remember the time I laced my feet into a pair of Colin's old working boots and followed the track down to the farm dump, a mound of debris that had grown up around the chassis of a broken vehicle in layers of wire and rusting tins, corrugated iron, shattered glass and flies. I'd gone there before your grandfather did because when he came, it would be with an empty grain sack and length of baling twine and deaf ear to the mewling as he bundled up a nest of tabby kittens on his way to the dam. The yabbies would work their way through the sack, Colin had said. The kittens would be a good feed for them, and, come Christmas Day, we'd make a meal of the yabbies. I chose quickly, without too much thought for what would happen to all the others. I picked the one with the longest white socks, but it was so young that when I looked I mistook its parts, and called a baby boy cat Shirley. I tried my best with Shirley, but he was feral through to the core and after the third time he woke Colin in the night with the sound of him crunching the bones of rabbit kittens under our bed, there wasn't much I could say or do to save him.

It wasn't long after Shirley had come and gone that I shifted Lad's feed bin from its place near the shearing shed to a post of the cottage fence which I could see through the kitchen window. I filled it with an extra helping of chaff and watched until he came. When at last he did, I went out to him, walking slowly and thinking of how I might scratch behind his ears and feel the worn-down velvet of his nose. Getting closer, I clicked my tongue at him. *Chuck chuck. Chuck chuck.* At the sound, he looked at me, his black eyes like wet billiard balls stuck into either side of his head. I could see the grey arches of his teeth as he continued to chew, and how the skin on the inside of his lips was salmon pink dappled with black. Flecks of lucerne clung to the rubbery skin of his muzzle like iron filings on a magnet.

He looked back at me, standing there in my white apron turned apricot from the orange-dusted air that had dried it on the clothesline, my hair coming loose from its bun. Again I made the noise with my tongue inside my teeth: *chuck chuck, chuck chuck.* It was meant to be a cheerful greeting in the only language that I knew for speaking to horses, but when he replied it was in English, in a voice that I do not think passed through my ears on its way right down to my core: *If your mother could see you now, her heart would break in two.*

But even if it were true that I'd been hasty, and even if I might have done better, I had done what I'd done and it couldn't be undone. If I'd been even as quick as Reggie, and not even necessarily quicker, it might have been me living down closer to town in one of those three little red-brick cottages that Mrs Kingsmith Snr had wanted built—at a respectable distance from the big house and from each other—so that none of her three boys would ever have to leave home. The cottages were pretty, with the same white window frames as the big house, and they even had green gardens out the front since the Kingsmiths could afford to buy in more water on top of what they got from the scheme.

I didn't ever really mind that it was Reggie who married Teddy, and I didn't covet that neat red-brick cottage, or even the geraniums in particular. Of all the things Reggie had and I didn't, it was her mother-in-law I might almost have been jealous about. Mrs Kingsmith was a tall woman with firmly set auburn curls and strong olive skin and if there was a carven quality to her long face, which remained uncannily still even when she spoke or laughed, it didn't matter because of the clear way her emotions showed in the narrow almonds of her green eyes. She managed her own angora goat stud and I had it from Reggie that she also did clever things with buying and selling shares. She treated all us young ones as if we were somehow her business, and I thought her warm and wise. It seemed all wrong to me that the daughter-in-law she'd been given to love was Reggie, who had a mother of her own still, while I had only Mrs Palfrey, who wanted nothing I had to give. When Colin and I told his mother that we were expecting Mark, she nodded resignedly and went back to worrying in the gloom behind her curtains.

When Reggie and I ended up side by side in the hospital with our newborn babies—she with Katharine, me with Mark—it wasn't envy that I felt about the expensive layette ('ecru', she said) that she'd ordered from an exclusive boutique back east, or about the soft pale blue gown with the satin trimmings that she wore while she nursed her baby daughter. I was happy enough with my lot: with my new baby boy and with the wildflowers Colin brought me; even if they were spindly, they were also delicate in their little glass vase alongside Reggie's towering hothouse arrangement.

Back at home, I stepped out of the ute with that posy tucked into the crook of my elbow and baby Mark wrapped up in a crocheted rug that my mother would have spotted from a mile off wasn't square. I'd never been much chop at crochet and the tension was loose and sloppy on the bottom edge, but better and tighter by the time I got up near the top, turning the whole thing into a rhomboid. I didn't mind and Mark couldn't tell, but there between the ute and cottage, switching at flies with his tail, was the horse with his eyes like black mirrors. I remember how I heard him inside of my ribs, as if my heart had grown its own mouth: *If your mother could see you now, her heart would break in two.*

Jimmy was born only ten months after Mark. I don't know why I didn't think to just send up a sky-writing plane to tell the whole district that I'd let your father back into my bed when Mark was barely a month old. I imagined the best of people calling me a rabbit and the worst of them calling me a whore. Can you imagine—one baby ten months old and the other newly born, and barely enough water to wash ourselves more than once in a week? And yet I had to spend my days soaking and rinsing nappies and watching what might as well have been gold for all the difference it made—it was so precious and rare—pouring away murky and brown.

People say their babies' early days pass in a blur, but I was never so lucky as all that. I don't think there's been a time in my life with edges so sharp as those years when the boys were little and I was home with them near enough to all alone. We felt flush for a couple of weeks after harvest, but for the rest of the year there was no money spare and everything that might have been just a little bit easier had to be done the hard way.

Although there was nobody but my parents-in-law at the big house to see, they were audience enough, and all the performance I could put on for them was the way my washing was hung. I had to do it with Jimmy bound across the front of me in a sling and Mark strapped in tight to his high chair out in the yard, and as I pegged I'd sing: *Four and twenty blackbirds* and *Hush, little baby, don't say a word* and *Oranges and lemons* just to try to keep them quiet for long enough to do it properly. Shirts are pegged at the armpits so the marks don't show. I knew that, of course, and how to hang the towels and the cleanest of the nappies on the outside strands of wire, screening off the inner wires where I could hang my bras and my underpants, although I pegged those at the crutch to hide what I could of that terrible, intimate yellowing. Those inside wires were also where I'd hang the towels whose side seams had burst and frayed, but even if they were hidden from the big house, the horse could still see. *If your mother could see you now, her heart would break in two*, he said. And, embarrassed at being caught out, I took down those towels and mended them wet before putting them back out on the line.

Shearing came around when Jimmy was barely three months and, although neither he nor Mark needed any less feeding, or made any fewer nappies between them, there was a huge batch of scones to bake each day for smoko. I made good scones, I know I did, and each time a tray of them came out of the oven tall and fluffy, I thought of my mother and that extra teaspoon of cream of tartar she'd taught me to add, and the lightning fast way she just barely scrambled together the buttery flour and the milk on the bench.

The cottage wasn't far from the shearing shed and it was nearly impossible to get my babies down for their daytime sleeps, the penned-up lambs screamed that loud for their mothers. I remember standing there at the kitchen sink with the scones all set out in baskets and the jam in bowls and the enamel mugs crammed into leaning towers on a tray on the bench. The big enamel teapot stood ready in the sink and the kettle was whistling. I poured the boiling water, knowing there was nothing I could do about Jimmy squalling in the other room; he was overtired, but he wasn't dying, so he was just going to have to wait. As if I needed the horse's bony face to appear in the window right at that moment, and glare down into those enamel mugs all stained orangey brown in rings down their insides. *If your mother could see you now, her heart would break in two.* My cheeks burned at the thought, and, although the shearers drank out of tea-stained mugs that day, it was the last time, even if it meant sometimes I had to stay up past midnight with a tub of bicarb of soda and an old toothbrush scrubbing the enamel until it gleamed.

If there's a God, then when he made me, he decided I'd be the type to learn each one of my life's hard lessons the hard way, and maybe not even the first time around. Stephen was born a week before Jimmy's first birthday, three months before Mark was two, so don't ever let anyone tell you that breastfeeding will do in place of precautions. I'd never even had a chance to get back into my monthly cycle before I was pregnant again, but I didn't want to believe it had happened so soon. When I took myself off to the doctor in town, it was with the hope that he'd come up with some other explanation for the sickness and the tiredness and the acid reflux that burned in my throat.

But I went home from the clinic with my fears all confirmed, and pegged out a bucket of nappies, crying as I inched along the wire, not knowing where the water would come from to wash half as many nappies again. Nor the physical strength. I'd lost so much weight bearing and feeding the first two boys that I looked, now, like a bag of bones with a disgusting, inflated belly. The doctor said it would be dangerous for me to feed the third baby myself, there was so little left of me. But where would the money come from to buy bottles or the formula to fill them?

I got to the end of the wire, the full length of it fluttering with flannel squares that nobody in their right mind would call perfectly white. I went around the end of the clothesline to hoist the full side high up into the drying air, and nearly tripped over the horse, standing there behind the flapping of the half-clean laundry. He looked at me then and peeled back his lips. *If your mother could see you now, her heart would break in two.*

ID

Nobody knew exactly how old that horse was. The best guess was that he'd been more than fifteen when he came as a worn-out hand-me-down to Colin as a boy, and twenty years had passed since then. Colin never paid the horse much attention although he was fond of the animal in a distant, careless way. It was supposed to happen once a year, but in truth it happened every other year or so that Colin tethered up the horse and filed his hooves and teeth. Just occasionally, but hardly ever, I'd see Colin pause on the path to stroke the old horse on the neck, mutter a word or two in his ear.

'How long do horses live?' I asked.

'You mean Laddie?' Colin shrugged. 'That old bugger'll go on forever.'

And it was true that in all the years I knew the horse, he didn't get to looking any older than when I'd first seen him, although perhaps that was only because there was nowhere left for him to go on that front: he already looked as old as he could look without being dead. I think that he might have become a little deafer, though, as there were times when I'd turn a corner and surprise him—in the cool of the machinery shed, or behind a stack of hay bales—and he would whicker at me, peevish and surprised. But if his hearing was imperfect, his eyesight remained keen. How hard I tried to always see him coming, and how hard I worked to give him as little as possible to see. If ever he peered, mid-morning, through the windows of the cottage, he would find all the boys' beds were made.

But even if the boys' beds were made, there were still the boys themselves. Whatever power my mother had for controlling six of them was not strong enough in me for only three. Those boys were so wild that their grandparents locked the doors to the big house, and suffered their company for brief Christmas lunches and Easter Sunday breakfasts. If Stephen was the softest of my boys, the one who used to kiss me on my eyelids and crawl into my bed in the night, that was all gone by the time he was four. Although I mended the knees of their jeans and scruffed hold of them for long enough to slap a wet cloth onto their faces before meals, the only real way I had to control those boys of mine was to call for Colin if he was near enough by, and he'd come, wearily unthreading his leather belt from his pants as he walked. Oh, the times that horse looked at them, filthy and feral and rude, and shook his ancient head. *If only your mother could see you now, her heart would break in two.*

And then, when Stephen was seven—a decent interval at last—there was you. You were with us, although I didn't even know it yet, on that day in early spring, when your father and your three brothers and I went for a picnic up on the 'hill' that I'd insulted your grandfather over, back when I was new to the farm. He'd mentioned the hill and I'd laughed without meaning to be cheeky; I really did think he was making a joke. Still, it was the biggest thing we had for a landmark and in a place this flat even an undulation lets you see for miles and miles.

There were months when the farm was nothing but tilled earth, and months when it was all hacked and dry and stubbled. It looked like money to us when the wheat was high and tawny, but the place was only ever really pretty for a couple of weeks in spring when the paddocks were green and the wildflowers thick in the places that couldn't be sown. There were quiet moments in spring, too—days when we'd have nothing much to do but watch over the growing crops, and hope for the best. I made a big deal of that picnic, making cakes and pies, and dressing the boys in good shirts and the better of their felt hats. I had in mind to take pictures, proof, of us happy and together and tidy.

Those photos were the best part of that day. The sun shone through a thin layer of cloud that made the light too soft for strict shadows, yet strong enough to make the flowers bright and give a glow to the places where the granite showed through the dirt. But your father wasn't used to spending time with all of us at once, and he kept looking at me as if I ought to have a way of stopping Jimmy from whining every time it wasn't fair, and getting Mark not to wind up poor Stephen.

I'd wanted to stay there all afternoon while the boys wandered off and played. I'd wanted to sit with your father and sip wine, and wait until the big red kangaroos came out at dusk. Your father grew up here, but I didn't, and the way those big reds covered the width of those paddocks without ever touching more than a square foot of the earth beneath them was never going to seem ordinary to me. But none of that happened. Instead the boys hovered like blowflies and, although I held on for as long as I could, trying to jolly everyone into making it the way only I could see it should be, in the end I got a headache and packed away the food. In the car on the way back I sulked a little, not exactly because the picnic had been a disappointment, but because I couldn't imagine the day when it might be any different than the way it was.

That was what I was thinking about when your father made a noise halfway between a shout and a curse word, and swerved the ute without warning through a torn-open section of fence, its broken wires strung with pale wisps of fleece. The boys whooped from in the back as the ute shuddered and jounced over ruts and ditches, and came to a stop in the middle of an untidy ring of dead ewes. We got out, all of us, and looked around. The sheep were a mess: the backs of their legs badly scoured, their eye sockets hollowed by birds. Not far away was a stand of low trees and shrubs: a banquet of spring greenery the sheep had forced the fence in order to reach, and threaded through the understory was a dainty shrub with sparse, waxy leaves and tiny blooms shading from red through orange to yellow.

'Bloody box poison,' your father said. 'Christ.'

There were twenty or more animals on the ground and later, once the corpses had rotted down a bit, Jimmy and Stephen made a tidy sum from plucking out and selling the long-stapled 'dead wool'. They got themselves nearly a bale. For now, though, all three of your brothers solemnly inspected the carnage, copying the pointless way their father nudged one of the beasts with the toe of his boot.

✄

Killing something always makes you think about life and what exactly it's made of. Not long after I moved to the farm I'd had to learn how to get a chook, all by myself, for dinner, so Colin showed me how. First you got a loop of baling twine and pulled it tight around a bird's neck. You hooked the other end of the looped twine onto a bent nail in the shed wall, then all you had to do was pull the chook's feet out as far as they'd go—pulling tight the string and the bird, both—and that way the chicken couldn't shrink its head back down into its shoulders and the neck would be all nicely stretched over the top of your chopping block.

The hatchet we had was small and sharp, and afterwards I'd turn my face away from the headless bird that I still had by the feet, waiting for the blood to stop squirting and the wings to stop flailing against the air and the side of my skirt. Instead I'd look at the little floppy head left lying there on the chopping block, or sometimes it would have bounced down onto the ground, and always it would occur to me that no matter how sorry I felt, there was nothing now that could be done to reverse it. There was no amount of wishing or wanting that could join that head once again to that body, and no amount of regret that could restart the thing I had stopped. Life didn't come in any form that you could pump back into a limp body through a mouth or a beak. It seemed a strange oversight to me that we could control the process only too well in one direction, but not at all in the other.

I had these same thoughts when I killed the horse, only it was worse because it took so much longer than with a chook. I didn't do it right after the sheep, of course. I waited a while, months, until the day of the picnic seemed long gone. On the day I chose, the horse watched me tip his ration of chaff back into the forty-four-gallon drum it had come from, and at the time I half thought that even if I made him hungry he'd still be too clever to start on the sheaves of foliage I'd put in his feed bin instead. But that plant must have tasted good to most animals because he got into it straight away. I watched him as he ate the way he always did, pulling back his lips so that his teeth might nip off those waxy, spear-shaped leaves, those pretty little sunbursts of blossom.

I almost wanted to stop it when the horse began to groan and whinny. It might not have been too late to call the vet. But I didn't. Nobody was there except myself to make me keep watching from the front veranda when the horse fell to the ground writhing and screaming, nor when he went into convulsions, his legs striking out at nothing, bloodied faeces streaming from his back end. The boys were off at school, their bikes tangled in a pile inside the corrugated iron lean-to that your father built for them down at the road, where the bus used to stop morning and night. And you, you were in my belly still. I don't know exactly how long it took, but thankfully the horse was still by the time those three bikes came skidding back in to the dust of the yard.

'The horse is dead,' I said to Colin when he got home right on dusk.

And all he said was, 'Where?'

Through the kitchen window I pointed to the place where gravity had been doing its work for the past few hours. All the sagging parts of the horse's body had been pulled earthwards, and when your father went out and walked a circle around the carcass, it looked hardly any thicker than a pelt rug at his feet. He crouched down beside it for a moment, took off his hat and ruffled the few strands of hair that still lay across the top of his scalp. Then he came back inside and sighed.

A horse is a large thing to bury in a place made of dry, stony earth. But not far from the cottage, just beyond the water tank, was an old, dead gum that needed to come down, so Colin and his father decided on a pyre. It took them half a day to fell the tree and chop it to pieces. Then they scooped up the horse's body in the bucket of the tractor and doused it in a whole jerry can of diesel. The fire burned all day and all night, and it left behind it a great, black circle on the earth. I wouldn't have said I was happy, but as I washed the smell of fire and meat from Colin's clothes and the boys', I thought that it would be the end of it.

But I was wrong, because now the horse was dust, and now the horse was ash. The horse was underfoot and the horse was in the air. The horse was particles all about me; I had breathed him into my lungs. I hate to think that I breathed him into you. I did what I did because I thought to do away with the horse, but instead I made it so the horse was everywhere, although its voice had now dropped to a whisper. *If your mother could see you now* . . . I've lived with it for all of your life.

You came into the world nearly twenty years ago now, with a full head of hair, a soft little cap of jagged blackness, and your eyes have never changed from that rich, precious blue. I called you Emma, the way I'd known I would, ever since I read that book at school. I wanted nothing ever to vex you.

Two days ago you came home, for a weekend, for a visit, to collect the very last of your things. Your leaving—this long, drawn out leaving—has been, for me, like a death. Although I've known of course, from the minute you were born, that it was coming, and even though it's been all the years of boarding school since you've lived with us here every day, there's still no way that I ever could have prepared myself for this pain that comes, right here, right now, at the end.

You came home this time with your dark hair grown longer still, and that proud flash in your blue eyes stronger than ever, making me want to slap you and kiss you at once. There's no reason you'd know how I felt in the days leading up to you coming, the little catch every time I walked past your bedroom: exactly the way you'd left it, only tidy. But it was just like you to come a whole day earlier than you said, to turn up when I was out, and when none of what I was doing was important or couldn't wait. It was only the post and my library books, and when I got back there was Robbie's car in the driveway and you two in the kitchen helping yourselves to cool drinks and ice. I'd bought Pimm's—it was in the liquor cabinet—and I wanted to have it all ready in the big green glass jug with fruit slices and tall glasses set out on a tray, and now you'd caught me in my old day dress and my hair not done. I got out of the car and the wind blew, stirring up that damned horse where he lay in the dust. *If your mother could see you now . . .*

On my way to my bedroom I walked past the open door to your room and there on your bed was your bag, and the arms and legs of your clothes already climbing out through the open zipper, stretching out over the coverlet, making their way back to their home on the floor. And on the foot of the twin bed in your room lay Robbie's case, neatly closed but just lying there as if he expected to sleep in your room alongside you. A breeze pushed a tasselled branch of tiny gumnuts against the window making a light scratching sound on the glass. *If your mother could see you now . . .*

I suppose there are modern ways of doing things, words that you can learn out of books to say so that you get it right every time, but I did what my own mother would have done and lifted that case of his off the bed and palmed away every trace of the imprint it had left in the candlewick, tugged at the bedspread edges all around to get it back straight. I carried his case down to the cottage and put it on the bed that I'd made up for him there and I knew that my face had got all tight while I was doing it and that it was still that way when I said to him, 'Robbie, you'll find your things at the cottage down the way'. And please don't think I didn't see that look that passed between you two, then. Don't ever think I miss the triumphant shine in your face each time I push you a fraction of an inch in the direction I already know you're wanting to go.

So now I watch you walk the rusted gravel of the driveway to Robbie's car sitting there with all its doors open like wings in the heat. I'm at the doorstep waving, and there is something I want to say to you but my tongue is locked, and, anyway, I do not know exactly what it is. I almost say 'don't listen to horses, they lie', but what sense would that make to you? I almost say 'I love you', but those are the words that are on all the Hallmark cards and in all the songs and such heavy use has worn away their substance; so light, as easily snapped as paper streamers, they seem to me these days. And although 'I love you' its perhaps the biggest part of what I want to say to you, it's still not even close to all.

You're walking with the smaller of your suitcases in your hand because your Robbie is gentleman enough to carry the larger one and I cannot see through the leather of either case to know which are the resentments, the injuries, the warnings, that you have packed away in the creases of your blouses, the hollows of your shoes. I do not yet know, and maybe never will, the ways in which I have damaged and disappointed you. I do not know myself what I have buried inside of you that will needle and bite and nag when you turn this way or that, and I cannot be sure that if I heard my own voice inside of you, I would even recognise its sound. But I do know that I'm standing here, that you're walking away, and that my heart is breaking in two.

acknowledgements

THANK YOU TO all my friends for listening and responding to my infernal yap. Thank you, Joanna Richardson, for being this book's first, perfect reader. Thank you, Colin Varney, for wielding the picky pen. Thank you, Robyn and Adrian Colman, for finding me the right music, and thank you, Julia Gibson, for letting me sit in on some yoga. Thank you, Nancy and Peter Godfrey, for taking me to 1958, and thanks to you too, Johnny the horse. The wise men to whom I refer on p. 6 might have been John Hurt, or Anthony Minghella, or both of them together. I gratefully acknowledge the lasting influence of *Jim Henson's The Storyteller*. Bless you, Annette Barlow, for your saintly patience, and thank you, Christa Munns, for the final polish. Writing would be so much harder without your practical help, Mary Mitchell, Peter Wood and

Jenny Wood—so, thank you. John Godfrey: someone once told me that you were the best bloke God ever shovelled guts into and I think they were right.